ISBN-13: 978-1-7337467-2-4

MacCulloch Castle Ghosts

Book Two

Silent Night

A MacCulloch Castle Christmas

M. KATHERINE CLARK

Other works by
M. Katherine Clark

The Greene and Shields Files
Blood is Thicker Than Water
Once Upon a Midnight Dreary
Old Sins Cast Long Shadows
Tales from the Heart, Novelettes

Love Among the Shamrocks Collection
Under the Irish Sky
Across the Irish Sea
On the River Shannon
The Land Across the Sea, an Emmet O'Quinn Short

Love Among the Shamrocks Collection the Next Generation
In Dublin Fair City
Song of Heart's Desire
Chasing After Moonbeams
You Don't Own Me – Coming Soon

The Wolf's Bane Saga
Wolf's Bane
Lonely Moon
Midnight Sky
Star Crossed
Moon Rise
Moon Song, a Companion Guide

Dragon Fire
Heart of Fire
Will of Fire
Born of Fire – Coming Soon

Sherlock Holmes Family
Soundless Silence, a Sherlock Holmes Novel
The Rest is Silence, an Edmond Holmes Novel

MacCulloch Castle Ghosts
Silent Whispers, a Scottish Ghost Story
Silent Night, a Scottish Christmas Ghost Story

Nollaig Chridheil, Everyone!

Chapter One

Ross

I glanced up from my laptop to see my new assistant, Iain knock at the open doorway.

"Sir," he greeted. The man was a little younger than me, but his dark hair was wildly curly and matching with his light blue eyes, he looked even younger.

After my mother's none-too-subtle encouragement to pick a male assistant after the last... incident involving Lorna, my previous assistant and her unrequited and misplaced affection, I advertised. I must have received a thousand resumes but something about Iain Mackenzie stuck with me after our initial call.

Today, instead of his usual pristine suit, he wore an ugly Christmas sweater, a string of flashing Christmas bulbs around his neck, and reindeer antlers attached to a Santa hat on his head.

"What are you wearing, Iain?" I questioned, leaning back in my desk chair.

He glanced down and beamed. "Too much? Miss Thompson said to go all out for the get together tonight."

"Ah, of course she did," my smile matched Iain's. "What else did my fiancée say?"

"Well," he debated. "She did say you would probably be a bit of a Scrooge and not have anything to wear, so she sent me down with this."

He produced another ugly sweater with a shirtless Santa lying in a very risqué pose before a Christmas tree with the words *I have a large package for you,* written on it. I stared at it for a moment, then burst out laughing.

"Seriously? Who thinks these sayings up?" I questioned.

"I'm fairly certain Miss Thompson had this one specially made." Iain beamed.

"I wouldn't put it past my mother to have helped her, either."

"Speaking of Lady Sutherland," Iain went on.

My eyes lit with excitement. "They're here?"

"They're here, sir. I have asked them to wait outside just in case Miss Thompson happened to walk by."

"Iain, you're a genius." I clapped him on the shoulder and headed for the door.

"Ehm, sir?" he called me back. I turned and he held up the sweater. "It is Miss Thompson's order I not let you out of my sight until I see you in this sweater."

I huffed a laugh but obligingly pulled off my current green cashmere sweater and slipped the ugly one on. I dared not look at myself in the mirror, I could only imagine from Iain's laugh.

"And the finishing touch," Iain said as he flicked a switch in the pouch of the tree. Santa's right eye winked as the lights on the tree he was laying in front of, twinkled.

"As if it couldn't get any more humiliating," I chuckled.

"Oh, I am sure it can," Iain replied. "I noticed Miss Thompson pulling out his and hers elf hats complete with oversized ears."

"Jaysus," I grunted. "The things I do for love."

Iain grinned. "I am so glad to not have that issue."

"Yet," I answered. "My future wife wants everyone happy and will soon turn her matchmaking sights on you, Mackenzie. Make no mistake." I laughed as the poor man swallowed hard and a look of pure distaste crossed his face.

Heading out the office door, I hurried to the entry and opened the heavy oak doors. The group of people that greeted me turned, and I was soon swept away in hellos and squeals of delight when certain ones saw my sweater.

Nikki Thompson and I had been engaged for just over ten months and had yet to have our actual engagement party. Apart from a quick family get together a couple days after I proposed, we were too busy to have a proper one. Both of our latest books had reached bestsellers lists across Europe and America, so she was barely home during her long five-month book tour when I had to find Iain, keep writing my next novel, and deal with the media. I decided it was time to announce who I was to the world and in early summer in an interview with *The Scotsman* and *The Times*, Elliot Ross, bestselling romance writer revealed he was in fact, Ross, fifteenth Baron and Laird of Sutherland, former world renown playboy and fiancé of Nikki Thompson, honorary citizen of Scotland and holder of Edinburgh City keys. Since then, I had all sorts of fan and hate mail. Fortunately, Iain also minored in Public Relations and helped smooth some of the issues.

After that, I went on a whirlwind author tour for four months. Nikki and I only had one overlapping month where we got to see each other. It was nice to have my fiancée home and no big plans until the new year.

The last year had been hard enough for both of us. So when she lay in my arms one evening about three weeks ago, and tears dripped onto my chest, I knew I would grant her anything. She missed her family and friends, Angus, the adventure with the Pride. Nikki made it clear it was nothing to do with me, which made me breathe easier, but it didn't help that she was missing her father and friends. At that moment, I vowed to make our engagement party one she would never forget. That meant I had Iain on flight and car reservations while I worked with our friends and family to get them to MacCulloch to surprise her at our castle employee Christmas and Holiday party.

As her father, my mother, my cousin Graeme, his mother Marilyn, Nikki's two best friends Jess and Brit, and three of our previous guests stood out in the slowly dropping cold, it was a wonderful reunion.

"Damn our girl is lucky," Chad, our American best friend who worked closely with us while Nikki strove to find the Highland Pride a few months ago, eyed my ugly sweater. "Just how large of a package are we talking about, Santa?"

"And you want to know this why, babe?" his husband questioned. I had only met Frank once before, but I immediately liked the shrewd doctor. Anyone who can keep up with Chad's endless, but meaningless flirtation, got a positive mark in my book.

"I like to keep my options open, silly. Besides everyone wants to know what in Santa's sleigh," Chad winked at us both.

"All I can say is, I am certain if he is like his father, there's nothing Nikki needs to worry about," my charming, though tactless, mother added her two cents.

Turning to Travis Thompson, Nikki's father and my mother's fiancé, I sighed. "I'm sorry."

"I'm not," Travis teased. "Your father gave your mother you and that makes my daughter very happy. No jealousy here, son." He winked. "Besides, I have my own endowment she's not talking about."

I groaned. There were some things a son never wanted to know and that was definitely at the top.

"I say, Sutherland," James Whitaker, one of our more famous authors who joined us at MacCulloch annually for our author's retreat, stood next to his wife Jenn, also a well-renown author, said. He was my new best friend for changing the subject. "I was a tad worried when you mentioned it was an ugly sweater evening. Jenn vowed to get me the most risqué sweater, but I think you win."

"It wasn't my choice, James," I answered.

"Still, Nikki has good taste," Jenn said eyeing me up and down. "The sweater isn't bad either."

We all chuckled but I was saved by Iain's subtle clearing of his throat. I turned to look up at him standing on the steps to the main entry.

"Sir," he began. "All of our guests' rooms are ready. Miss Thompson is still typing away in her room so for the sake of the surprise, I would highly suggest moving quickly."

"Indeed, thank you, Iain." He stepped back just enough to enter the lobby. "Now, you all know what I'm hoping for," I spoke to our friends. "I know Nikki will be so happy to see you all. Jess, Brit," I turned to Nikki's best friends and her ex's sisters. "You two are on the second floor in two rooms facing each other. But you are the closest to Nikki's room so be sure to keep quiet." I winked.

"Not to worry," Jess squealed grabbing her boyfriend's arm. "I can be so quiet."

"Not in my experience," Graeme, my cousin and best friend and Jess's boyfriend piped up, a salacious grin on his face. She giggled but put a finger to her lips shushing him.

"Chad, Frank, you are in Chad's old room. Thought it might bring back good memories."

"The best now I have my hubby with me," Chad teased pulling on Frank's arm and bouncing up and down. The air was getting colder, and I could smell snow on the horizon.

"James, Jenn same room as last time. Marilyn, your usual. Mum, Travis, same as always. I've made sure there's a welcome basket in there for each of you. A little thank you for flying out here during the Christmas rush. Let's get you in, it's freezing."

Everyone hurried in after me and Iain passed out room keys.

"Remember, as soon as the clock strikes six," I reminded them. "All of you gather outside the library bar. Iain will leave the room just before and make sure you're all ready before opening the doors."

"Then we shout surprise!" Jess squealed and everyone's unison *shh* made her grimace and mouth *sorry.*

I watched them all hurry to their rooms and looked back at Iain. "Champagne on ice?"

"Ready and waiting."

"Wait staff all prepared?" We had hired an event staff so our staff wouldn't have to work that evening.

"As instructed. I spoke with Marcus, too," he mentioned

my chef. "He has passed the reins over to the hired chef and they are on schedule, and everything will be ready to pass once we have your orders."

"Oh brilliant," I said. "Now, to pry my woman away from her laptop and convince her to come downstairs with me in half an hour."

"That I cannot help you with, sir," Iain answered. "All I can say is, *you who are about to die, I salute you.*"

Chuckling, I waved him off and headed up the stairs to her room. Though it was true, never get between a writer and their ideas, computer, storyline, or characters, I knew my woman. The future Lady Sutherland would be happy to know we're finally celebrating our engagement, even though our wedding was set for first of the year. Smiling at the thought of her being my wife, I knocked and opened the door to be greeted with a frustrated groan and a curse.

"Dammit it all to hell," Nikki spat and angrily clicked around on her computer just to slam the lid shut and huff.

Chapter Two

Nikki

I had a problem. A huge, major, big-time problem. The black cursor was blinking at me on an empty white page.

Writer's block.

The dreaded time of no inspiration, no idea, and no voices of characters begging to have me tell their story.

I had that once before in my career, just after my ex-boyfriend broke up with me. I went to a writer's retreat in MacCulloch Castle north of Edinburgh about fifty miles and met a ghost. Angus MacPherson. My longtime distant grandfather and friend. Just thinking about him made my chest ache. I missed him horribly. My last book was about our adventure together to find the Highland Pride, a precious ring designed as the original symbol of Scotland by Robert the Bruce himself and given to William Wallace when he was named Protector of Scotland. It came to my family during the battle of Stirling Bridge and had been passed down generation to generation until it was stolen just before the Battle of Culloden.

It was a journey that brought me to my future and Ross, and one I would never forget. How I wished I could see Angus again. He was the one who helped push Ross and me together. Nothing in my life was as exciting anymore. I felt my world wasn't my own. Ross and I went our separate ways more often than not and now that the wedding was nearly planned, I wasn't sure it was what I wanted. Oh, I wanted Ross, don't get me wrong. But I wasn't sure if I wanted the fuss of the huge wedding I always thought I wanted. I would be content with just our friends and family and calling on one of them to be ordained by some website.

Not that we had many friends anymore. Too busy. But I missed them. Jess and Brit. Chad. Even thinking of his handsome milk chocolate face and violet eyes made me smile. Graeme and Gerard, Ross's cousins, although we hadn't seen Gerard for over a year. He had left after his mother revealed their father was Ross's uncle. Fortunately, he had called his mother for her birthday, so we knew he was alive, but he refused to tell us where he was or to come home.

"Enough reminiscing, Nikki Thompson," I chided myself. "Write." I turned up my YouTube playlist of Celtic instrumental Christmas music and tried to write something. My editor was clamoring for a new idea, new pages, something, and I had a grand total of zilch to offer.

Looking out my window to the maze garden in the back of the property illuminated in the security and ambient lights of the ugly sweater party I was happy to organize for our Employee Holiday Party, I gazed further out to the copse of trees and to the old, rusted water pump that once indicated Angus' unmarked grave. Though I could not see it in the dim light, the snow from the other day was melting in patches and covered the ground in an eerie glow. It grew dark quicker in winter and though the clock only read five thirty, it had been nighttime for almost an hour.

Humming along to the instrumental of my favorite Christmas song, I absently let my fingers walk over the keyboard. Words didn't come easy, but I was happy to see sentences forming. After a short time, I paused and scrolled up to read over what I had written.

It was a load of shite.

Groaning in frustration, I wanted to hit Ctrl A and then delete the entire thing, but it was the most I had written in months and maybe with some tweaking it would be halfway presentable. I doubted it.

"Dammit all to hell," I cursed and, clicking save, slammed my laptop lid closed, huffing out a breath.

"Bad time?" I heard Ross say from the door. Spinning around in my chair, my lips immediately pulled into a grin when I saw his sweater.

"Just frustrated with my brain," I admitted when I realized I hadn't answered his question. "No idea is coming to me."

"It happens, babe, don't let it get you down." He stepped into the room and walked over to me. His hands gently coming down to massage my shoulders.

"Says the man with dozens of books out."

"Not quite dozens," he laughed. "You need to relax, Nikki. No idea is going to come to you and stick when you're this stressed."

"I know," I said. "But it doesn't help. I am happy for any sort of distraction... hence the sweater."

He chuckled and it was amazing how much that relaxed me. "Cocktails are going to be poured any minute." He whispered. "Come down with me?"

"Mm," I moaned. "Can we celebrate on our own?"

"Nope, not a chance," he answered. "Besides, you got me into this ugly sweater. You should see Iain. The staff are excited about it."

"I'd much rather stay in my room with my sexy Santa and his… package."

"*Large* package I think is the exact wording."

"It is. I picked it out specifically for you," I winked.

"I was the talk of the downstairs," he grinned. "But really, Nikki, come down and have a drink with me. If you hate it in an hour, we can discretely make our exit. We owe our employees that much."

The music mix switched to *Auld Lang Syne* and the sound of the penny whistle playing the old Robert Burns poem filled me with happiness.

"I can't refuse when I know how much work has gone into this. I'm sorry I'm being selfish."

"Hey now, none of that," he said. "You're not being selfish. You're exhausted, love."

"So are you," I replied, seeing the faint dark circles under his eyes.

"Aye, but that's because my fiancée keeps me up at night," he leaned down and brushed his lips against mine.

No matter how many times my Scotsman kissed me, I still melted.

"I love you," I said softly.

"I love you, too," he answered. Another soft kiss, and he pulled away. "Come down. Where's your ugly sweater?"

"In my closet," I grinned excited to share my choice. Pulling it out, I yanked it on, my back still turned to him so he couldn't see the front and then dramatically turned to show him.

"'Santa likes me naughty... list,'" Ross read as he chuckled. His Scottish accent giving the right inflection on the right word. "That's right, baby. I like you naughty."

Biting my lip as my smile grew, I bounced over to him and kissed him quickly. Pulling back, I plunked a Santa hat on my head complete with large elf ears and pushed a button. Ross exclaimed surprise as the hat started playing a rock 'n' roll Christmas song and the top of the hat danced.

"That's amazing," he beamed. The lights of the fireplace and Christmas tree standing in the corner of the room, reflected in his eyes and made me fall even more in love with him. "Come on, love. Let's go have fun."

Right as he said it, music started from downstairs, loud enough for us to hear it, though my door was open. All thoughts of deadlines, editors, blank pages, and non-ideas, gone, I took Ross's hand and we walked together out of the room, down the hall, and into the library bar where our staff had gathered.

Ross

She had no idea what I had planned, and it made me... giddy. A grown man. It was laughable. I shook my head and chuckled.

"What?" she questioned. Turning to her, I realized my mistake.

"Just seeing the lights twinkle and Santa wink at me on my sweater," I covered.

"Do you like it?" the look in her eye made me laugh.

"I love it," I answered.

"Oh good, I honestly was a little worried."

"Why?"

"Well, I know how it can look but I fell in love with it immediately and wanted you to wear it. After I bought it, I wondered how you would feel."

I stopped her and turned to face her. "I love it, Nik, honestly. Yes, it's a tad risqué but that's what makes it fun and a perfect ugly Christmas sweater."

"Good, you would tell me if you hated it, right?"

"You know I would," I replied and kissed her hand.

"Okay," she smiled. Then, glancing over my left shoulder, her eyes fixed on the portrait I had commissioned for her birthday. The portrait of Angus MacPherson and his second wife Elizabeth had been taken away and stored in the vaults in Sutherland Manor as I refused to have anything reminding Nikki of that evil woman. The new one I had commissioned was of Angus and his first wife Riona, who Nikki looked exactly like. She even sat for the portrait. "I wonder if he's okay."

"Angus?" I questioned. She nodded and a cloud descended over her eyes. "You've been thinking about him a lot, Nikki. I don't like the nightmares you've been having recently."

Her eyes locked with mine as she tilted her head questioningly. "What nightmares?"

"You don't remember?"

She shook her head. That was odd, she'd woken up screaming Angus's name the last three days. I studied her and wondered if I should have mentioned it sooner.

"You never talk about it," I explained. "But you call out for Angus, and it wakes you up."

"Why don't I remember this?" she worried her lower lip.

"I'm not sure," I answered.

"If I do it again, could you make sure to ask me?"

"Of course," I stroked her chin with my knuckles. "I love you, Nikki Thompson."

"I know you do, Laird Sutherland," she replied, reaching up to nuzzle my nose and kiss me. "I love you so much, Ross. But I am worried. This writer's block isn't normal. My dreams. All of it. Am I... am I going crazy?"

"No, darling," I stated. "It happens. You've had an amazing adventure and wrote about it. Now, you are in *post book tour* haze. It's only natural for you to have some doubts. Trust me. I know what I'm talking about, love. You'll get through it. I'll help you in any way I can. You are an amazing writer, Nikki. Sometimes amazing writers need time off. I don't want you to worry about anything tonight. Have fun. That's all I ask."

"I will do my best."

"And your best is always incredible." I took her hand again and walked her into the library bar where our staff of thirty waited.

It was the last day they worked for the Christmas holiday. We had no guests other than the surprise ones, but I worked it out with Marcus, and he had left a couple cooked hams, turkeys, side dishes, and breakfast items we could warm up during our stay. The local village was also an option and the pub stayed open until Christmas Eve.

I always looked forward to the last day of MacCulloch for the holiday season as it was a good time for me to get to know who worked for me and allowed them the pleasure of having the open bar, good food, and gifts I purchased or had purchased for them. I usually joined Mum at Sutherland Estate the day after, but she had been busy closing the house up. She was lonely up there by herself and would soon live full time at MacCulloch with Travis, Nikki, and me.

Planning for the holiday party usually began the first of October with a short break for Samhain and the Solstice, but that year, Nikki took the reins as I was on my North American book tour. It was her idea to make it an Ugly Christmas Sweater theme and have more traditional Christmas foods blending our two cultures: American and Scottish. I looked forward to the sugar cookies and eggnog but also mince pies and mulled wine.

Entering the library bar, our staff greeted us with a "Happy Christmas!" and applause along with the general gaiety our sweaters brought. After giving handshakes and hugs, Nikki and I reached the front where a small stage was set for a round of Christmas karaoke. Turning to our staff, I started the welcome speech.

"It is so wonderful to be able to share another Christmas Holiday with you all. Our little tradition is one I look forward to every December and I am so glad to be able to share it with my fiancée. She's had some," I purposefully glanced down at my sweater. "*Interesting* ideas along the way, but I wouldn't change it for anything. It gives us all a little something to enjoy. We have some wonderful treats for you all and I do believe a little something under the tree for each of you. Cabs are lined up outside starting at eight and paid for to get you all home. Drink however much you'd enjoy without worry. I, ehm," I looked down for a moment then smiled. "I know I can speak for Nikki and myself when I say we have absolutely the most amazing support in the world. You all have done so much, and we can't thank you enough for everything. Nikki? Do you want to say a few words?"

Nikki nodded and stepped up beside me. "I agree with

everything Ross just mentioned. We could not do any of this without all of you. You are all so dear to us. You have welcomed me with open arms and for me, that is the greatest gift. I can't thank you all enough for everything you do to make this hotel run smoothly. It is so wonderful to be able to call you all my friends. You have been a lifeline for me when I was missing Ross and my family and friends in America. Thank you all and Happy Christmas!"

There was a cheer as everyone toasted with the champagne that stood on the bar. Nikki and I toasted each other and our staff, and the party began.

We made it through three rounds of terrible karaoke and two rounds of not so terrible. Laughing the entire time with my staff, it was a wonderful time. There was a break in the singing just before six o'clock chimed on the grandfather clock. I couldn't contain my grin when Iain slipped out of the room.

"What's that smile for, Sutherland?" Nikki questioned.

I tried to school my features but to no avail. "Happy to have you by my side for Christmas, my love," I answered. "And I hope this year will be a year to remember." I deliberately looked over to the door as Iain opened it again. Nikki turned and gasped as everyone from earlier spilled into the room.

"Oh my god!" she squealed.

"Happy Christmas, my love. And welcome to our engagement party," I whispered.

She cried happy tears as she turned back to me and framed my face. Kissing me before our entire staff was not something I was used to, but I tuned out the hoots and cheers and kissed my fiancée before she pulled away with a quick "oh, I love you" and hurried to meet our family and friends.

Chapter Three

Nikki

"Oh my god!" I squealed again as I flung myself into my father's arms. I hadn't seen him in months. He and Jacqueline, Ross's mother, had gone up to Sutherland Estate for the September hunting season since Ross couldn't make it back from Boston in time. But they had decided to stay up there for a few weeks to close up the house. I missed them both terribly.

"We had to come back, sweetie," dad said as I embraced Jackie. "Ross told us you were a little sad and he wanted to celebrate your engagement finally, so naturally we hopped in the car and drove down."

"Thank you so much. I have missed you both so much!"

"We've missed you too, darling," Jackie replied. Her naturally proper English accent shining through. "You could have easily come up to be with us if you needed to get away. You are going to be mistress of Sutherland Estate when you and Ross marry. I know what writer's lives are like. But I missed you!"

"I missed you too, Jackie, but you're right and there was just so much to do here."

"And you've done a fine job, honey," Chad's voice came from beside me.

"Oh my god," I cried even harder, though they were happy tears when I saw him. "I can't believe you're here!" I threw my arms around him and embraced him, loving the tight squeeze he gave me.

"God, I've missed you, babe," he said. "It has been too long. Did you get prettier?"

"Way too long. It is so good to see you, you flirt."

"It's good to see you, Nikki," Frank, Chad's husband said standing beside him. "If anyone can help me keep this man in line, it's you."

"Any time." I embraced Frank. "I can't believe it's been three months since I saw you."

"More like four," he answered. "It was end of summer when you reached Maine."

I had stayed with Frank and Chad when I was on my New England leg of my signing tour and loved their nautical themed transformed old lighthouse home. I also got to know Frank a lot better and was so glad to call him a friend.

"God, I can't believe it!"

"Us neither!" Jess and Brit stepped into my embrace and held on tightly. Though I had just seen Jess about a month ago when she had flown to Edinburgh to meet Graeme for his birthday, it was still wonderful to see both of my friends. They were sisters of my ex-boyfriend Darren, who I found out had started dating his new editor and seemed serious about her. When Jess had let it slip a month ago, I won't lie I had a moment of questioning what did she have that I didn't have, but then I looked over at Ross, sitting in our study with me, hard at work on his new novel, and all my thoughts vanished.

I embraced James and Jenn, so happy to see them again after nearly ten months. Of all thirteen authors who attended the tenth annual League of Extraordinary Writer's Author's Retreat the year before, I counted Chad, Marilyn, James, and Jenn as my personal friends.

"I'm so happy to see all of you!" I wiped my tears and leaned back into Ross's chest when I felt him come up behind me. "Thank you for coming. And thank you for arranging it," I turned to Ross. He kissed my neck and tweaked the bauble on my elf hat.

"Iain helped me with a lot of it."

Iain stood proudly to the side, his hilarious ugly sweater making me laugh. "Thank you, Iain. It means a lot."

"Anything for you, Miss Thompson. You light up our lives and I am glad to be able to work for you," Iain said.

"Ehm, you work for me, Iain," Ross teased.

"No, I don't," Iain grinned.

Ross chuckled and shook his head. "I suppose he's right."

"Come in, come in," I coaxed. "Sorry to have railroaded you in the doorway. There's champagne, wine, and beer along with our mixed drinks. The bartenders are strictly forbidden to work today so you have free reign of the bar, but we have hired a couple bartenders so if there's a drink you'd like mixed, let them know."

"I'll just have a beer," dad said. "Jackie, love?"

"*Scotch and,* for me," she answered ordering her usual

Scotch and soda but calling it by the old nineteen-thirties name I had seen in movies.

"Babe?" Graeme offered.

"I'll take a champagne," Jess answered giving him a quick kiss. "Thanks."

Graeme grinned and as he headed over to the bar, the fresh hickey on his neck was revealed just above the top of his sweater collar. Looking back at Jess, I laughed at her naughty grin. Clearly whenever they had arrived, they had not wasted any time.

When all the men had gone to get drinks, I realized Brit had been left out. She was the only one of the group who didn't have a date... actually she had never had a date. I never understood why, she was so pretty and sweet but with Jess as a big sister, I often wondered what sort of contest and competition they would have had.

"Brit, what can I get you?"

"Nothing," Brit answered though I could see the slight hurt in her eyes when none of the men had offered to get her something. That was something I would be speaking to Ross about as soon as possible. "I'll get it myself. I always do." The mumbled words nearly broke my heart.

There had been one guy last year and earlier this year she had talked about. But I had the impression it was unrequited and soon after, I was proven correct when she stopped talking about him altogether. I was about to go after her when Jess took my arm and herded me over to where Jenn, Marilyn, and Jackie sat near the fireplace.

"Darling," Marilyn greeted as if I hadn't just greeted her a few seconds ago. I beamed. She was truly one of my favorite people. "Sit by me. Tell me, has your man given any hints about the honeymoon?"

"He said it's somewhere warm but that's it," I answered.

"I bet it's the South of France," Jackie stated.

"Or the Bahamas," Marilyn offered.

"Ugh, the Bahamas are amazing," Jess replied. "Graeme took me over the summer. Seriously, the best place ever. Do all Scotsmen get frisky after a Mai Tai?"

I laughed along with the other ladies, but something caught my eye and I watched. Iain approached Britney and offered a glass of champagne. She looked up at him and smiled slightly. He said something but I was too far away to make it out and I was never good at reading lips but whatever it was, Brit nodded, and they moved to one of the cocktail tables standing between the two doors to the room. They spoke together, Iain smiling and his eyes twinkling. I wondered... my matchmaker mind whirling.

"Nikki? Nik?" I heard Jess call. "Earth to Nikki Thompson soon to be Nikki Sutherland." I looked over.

"Sorry, miles away."

"That brings up a good question," Jess went on as if I hadn't said anything. "Are you going to change your name after you get married?"

"Oh, well, um yeah. Ross and I haven't really talked about it. But yes," I answered.

"Pity," Jess shook her head. "A woman needs to remain independent. Why bow to the patriarchal society? I mean it's everywhere so why should we have to stroke their egos?"

"Jess, I love you and your ideals but I'm marrying a titled Laird. I may continue to use Nikki Thompson as my pen name since everyone knows me like that, but I will be Nikki Sutherland everywhere else."

"*Lady* Nicole Sutherland," Jackie winked. "And though I agree with female empowerment, there is little we need to do to make our men see our way of thinking. Though I am of a different generation than you, my dear, I believe the more we push, the harder it will be for us. We already have a female First Minister, a female Prime Minister, and we may very well have a female President one of these days, we women hold the highest positions of authority. Let us prove we got there on our merit not simply because we are women. Once we conquer that, then we have reached true equality and dismantled the patriarchy, and they'll never know."

"Here here," Marilyn agreed.

"I never thought of it like that," Jess said.

"Oh, I've had many years to think on it. Don't forget it was Mari's and my generation who burned our bras."

"Who's burning bras?" Dad asked walking up and offering Jackie her drink. Ross and Graeme came up next and gave Jess and me our drinks.

"Speaking of our generation's fight against the patriarchy, love," she answered giving him a kiss.

"Ah, damn, I was kinda hoping we were going to have a party," Dad teased and sat beside her, his arm lining the couch.

"I have plenty I can burn just for you, Trav," she replied. Dad grinned but sipped his scotch.

I loved seeing my dad so happy and I loved Jackie. Their relationship was a surprise, but I never discouraged it. Dad deserved to be happy, and I was honored when he asked for my blessing before proposing. I couldn't say yes fast enough and helped him plan the perfect time.

The thought of marriage and love caused me to glance back to where Iain and Brit were still deep in conversation. Sending a silent prayer up to the heavens, I hoped he wouldn't hurt my friend.

Ross

The party was winding down after a couple hours. Some of the staff had gotten their bonus checks from under the tree and thanked us before wishing us a Happy Christmas and heading out. Soon, it was only a handful of the staff left and our group of family and friends. I glanced around and smiled, though my heart was still somewhat heavy not seeing Gerard. My other best friend had left before Nikki had found the Highland pride over a year ago and though his twin brother Graeme and I went looking for him after a couple months, it was like he had vanished completely. The one saving grace we had was he had called Marilyn, his mother, for her birthday but refused to say where he was or what he was doing.

Growing up, Graeme and Gerry were my best friends, it was only after thirty-two years we found out we were, in fact, cousins. My father Connor's younger brother Owen had drugged and taken advantage of Marilyn, fathering the twins. After Gerry had found out what his father had done, he had left. I wished him back with all my heart. We were always the three musketeers, the three of us were inseparable. It was strange not having him with us.

Then, as if my thoughts had conjured him, the door opened, and Gerard walked in.

He froze.

We froze.

Conversation died.

"Gerard?" Marilyn gasped.

"Ger?" Graeme questioned.

"I'm sorry," he began. "I didn't realize you were having a

party. I'll go." He turned.

"Don't you dare," I ordered. He stopped and turned back. I stood from my perch on the arm of the couch nearest to Nikki. Stalking toward him, almost afraid he would bolt, and I wouldn't get answers, I approached as calmly as I could, but my hands were shaking.

"I didn't mean to interrupt," he tried again. "I would have gotten a room at the village inn, but it was booked through Christmas."

"You bastard," I reached him and yanked him into my arms. He stiffened as if surprised, but I thumped him on the back and tightened my hold. "Where the hell have you been?"

He didn't answer and I pulled back to look at him. His usually soft brown eyes and playful but serious nature was gone. In its place was something unfamiliar, something dark, almost dead. Whatever happened to him, whatever he had done, wherever he had been, had changed him. My best mate, my cousin, was gone. In his place, stood a stranger.

"What happened to you?" I breathed.

Again, my answer was silence.

"Ger?" Graeme questioned. I nearly jumped. While I was observing the changes, Graeme had walked up behind me.

"Graeme," Gerry greeted his twin brother.

"Thank god," Graeme groaned and nearly pushed me aside as he pulled his brother into an embrace. As with mine, Gerry remained stiff as a board and did not hug back. "Where have you been? What have you been doing? I tried calling and calling. What the hell is wrong with you?"

"Nothing," Gerry spat. "I'm sorry I interrupted your party. I was only going to see if you had an extra room for the night. If not, I'll sleep in my car."

"Of course we have a room for you," I answered. "But tell us what happened first."

He turned those dead eyes on me, and I shivered. "If that is the stipulation, I'll find my car." He turned to leave again.

"Gerard," his mother cried. I didn't realize Marilyn was weeping behind me until I heard her wail. Turning to see my mum holding her shoulders, giving comfort, I looked back at Gerry. He had stopped midstride and his back rose and fell as he took a deep breath. He looked different from that angle too. Under his forest green sweater, his back had filled out more than it was before. He had more muscles than I remembered, and his legs looked like tree trunks captured in a pair of tight jeans. Again, I caught myself wondering what had happened to him. "Please, love."

Gerry's back rose and fell again, but a little more rapidly than before. "I'm sorry." He said softly but the two words were filled with emotion as he did not turn and walked down the hallway.

"Gerry!" I shouted after him. I started down the corridor when a flurry of dark auburn hair and ugly Christmas sweater zipped by me. "Britney?" I questioned.

"Let me talk to him," she threw over her shoulder. "He may listen to me."

"Why?" the soft but confused question left my lips, but she was past the check in counter and out the door following Gerry's trail, before the question reached her.

Chapter Four

Nikki

I was so very worried and confused... and surprised. Gerard hadn't been seen since the day trip we took to Angus MacPherson's old castle to find the Pride. And he just crashed Ross's and my engagement party. Don't get me wrong, I was happy to see him. Ecstatic in fact, but that didn't change my reaction. All of our reactions, honestly. I felt the worst for Marilyn. She wept as Gerry left without so much as a hello to his mother. That wasn't the Gerard Fergus I knew.

"He hates me," Marilyn wailed against Jackie's chest.

"I'm sure that's not true, Mari," Jackie said.

"He hates me, it's obvious. Oh dear god, I've lost him. My boy!" she wailed again.

"That son of a bitch," Graeme spat. "What the hell was he thinking? Damn idiot. The arsehole doesn't do so much as a phone call for a year and then waltzes in here large as bloody life and expects us not to have questions?"

Jess took her boyfriend's arm, but he promptly shook her off, too angry to be soothed.

"Can I be of any assistance?" Iain walked over to us.

"Thank you, Iain, but I don't think so," I said. "I'm not sure what is going to happen. Thank you so much for a lovely evening. You are all welcome to stay for as long as you would like." I addressed the remaining few employees, but the murmured assent was clear, they would all be leaving soon.

Ross came back into the room and Graeme walked over to him. "Anything?"

Ross shook his head. "Britney went to him."

"Brit?" Jess questioned. "Why?"

"She said she thinks he may talk to her," Ross explained.

A couple of the remaining staff hurried over to us and thanked Ross and me for a wonderful evening. Wishing us a Happy Christmas, we were alone, apart from Iain who looked terribly uncomfortable. No wonder. The girl he had been chatting with suddenly drops him and rushes after a complete stranger. I needed to know the history between Brit and Gerry. For her to believe he may listen to her, there was clearly something there.

Ross sat beside me and placed his arm around my shoulders, draining his remaining scotch. "I'm sorry, baby," he began. "Not the ending to our engagement party I was expecting."

"Oh Ross," I took his hand resting on my shoulder and kissed his knuckles. "I have had a wonderful evening and I am so happy Gerry is back. Yes, I think it's become a wee bit awkward, but that's life. We learn to take it in stride."

"I love you," he said.

"I love you, too," I answered and kissed him briefly.

"Jenn and I can head on up if you'd rather. This seems to be a family matter," James said.

"No, not at all," Ross replied. "You're welcome to stay, James. But we understand if you would rather leave. It wasn't expected and apparently quite the drama."

"We'll see you in the morning," Jenn offered.

"Breakfast will be ready around nine, if you're hungry before then, please feel free. The kitchen is ours for the remaining couple weeks. But Marcus has made sure we won't starve," I explained.

"Capital," James smiled. "So happy to be celebrating with you two. Thank you for having us."

"We can't wait to talk again," Jenn said. "See you all in the morning. Happy engagement party!"

After they left, Chad leaned over to me and took my hand. "How you holding up, honey?"

"I'm just worried about Gerry," I answered. "I wish he would talk to us."

"He looks like he's been through a war," Frank said. "I've seen that sort of dead look in my Veteran patients. My guess is, he's seen or done things he can't forgive himself for. But I'm no phycologist."

"Would it be better if we headed up too?" Chad asked. "We don't want to intrude on a family matter."

"You are family. You are welcome to stay but if you'd like to, we understand," I replied.

"Don't get me wrong, all this drama is delicious," Chad said. "But it might be better for it to remain family only. Though I was with you from the beginning of his whole thing."

"Chadwick," Frank whispered.

"All right all right," Chad sighed. "I know I'm in trouble when *Chadwick* comes out." He leaned forward again and kissed my cheek. "Keep me posted."

"Will do, thanks for being here tonight."

"Anything for my girl," he winked and let Frank hold his arm as he weaved a little from the drinks he had consumed and walked out of the room.

It was an agonizing few minutes, Marilyn weeping, Graeme pacing, and everyone silent until we heard the door open and Brit walked in followed by Gerry.

"You bastard," Graeme roared when he saw his brother.

"If I'm one then you are too," Gerry answered calmly. Almost too calmly.

Graeme stared at his brother. "What the bloody hell are you on about? What the bloody hell have you been doing and where the bloody hell have you been?"

"Isn't it obvious?" Gerry finally showed some emotion other than anger as he stood toe to toe with his brother. "I was tracking our father down and planning his murder."

The room went silent apart from the crackle of the fire's dying flames.

"You... what?" Graeme stammered.

"I tracked the bastard down. Owen Sutherland. I found him."

"Where is he?" Graeme demanded.

"Dead."

"Gerry?" Ross questioned. "You didn't..."

Gerry turned his cold eyes to Ross. "Didn't what? Kill him? You don't want a murderer in your house, Ross?"

"I want my friend back. I don't care what happened," Ross answered.

"I want to know what happened," Graeme stated. "Did you kill him?"

Gerry looked over at his brother. We all held our breath as we waited for his answer.

"No," he said firmly. "The bastard was already dead. Three years ago. Heart failure."

"How did you find that out?"

"I have my ways," Gerry answered.

"Why the hell did it take you this long to come back?" Ross demanded.

"Because I just found him two weeks ago," Gerry replied. "I had every intention of finding him and killing him. Ridding the world of a rapist once and for all. But he beat me to it. Stole that last little bit of revenge from me."

"Gerard," his mother breathed. He looked over at her and hurried to her side. Pulling her into a hug, Marilyn cried into his chest.

"I could never hate you, Mum," he said softly. "But I was so angry at the man who did that to you. You know how I get when I'm angry. I need to be alone."

"Where were you?" she hiccupped.

"For the first couple months, I was in my cabin in the woods. Just up there," he pointed out the window. "For the next few I was in Edinburgh looking through the archives, trying to find him. I hired a private investigator and everything. I tracked down the leads myself. None of them panned out."

"You were in the cabin?" Ross questioned. "We went there. It looked like no one had lived there for a while."

"That's what I wanted it to look like. I saw you both. I was in the woods, but I couldn't come back. I was far too angry."

"What calmed you?" I asked.

He glanced at Brit and then back to me. "A fresh perspective."

I looked over at my best friend seeing the tells, her cheeks tinged with pink and the nervous tick we never told her about, wringing the first knuckle of her left pointer finger. Something happened between them, I was certain.

"Look, all I can say is, I was angry, still am. I'm angry I did not get to avenge my mother, but I am back now. So, can we all just stop this?"

"Not by a long shot," Ross answered. "But it's after midnight. Perhaps we should table this until the morning. You're staying."

"I may have plans."

"You're staying." Ross's tone brooked no refusal. "Iain," he turned to his assistant. "You're staying another night, right?"

"If that's all right, sir," Iain said. "I'll leave for Invergordon first thing."

"That's fine," Ross answered. "Stay as long as you'd like or need. But get your bonus from under the tree."

"I got it earlier this evening. Thank you, sir," he bowed slightly.

"Good, then I think it's time we all go to bed."

Everyone followed Ross's order and headed up to their rooms. Before I left, I looked back to see Gerry still on the sofa where his mother had kissed his cheek. Brit was still standing by the doorway, and Iain stood near the bar watching. Unsure what was going on between them, I hoped it would work out.

Chapter Five

Ross

I had never been so angry and relieved in my life as I stalked to Gerry's room early the next morning. It had been over a year since I had last seen him, and I wasn't going to leave his room until I had some answers. But as soon as I reached the door, all questions died on my lips. I could hear muffled voices from behind the door. Glancing at my watch, it was just past seven in the morning. I hadn't been able to sleep but I didn't want to keep Nikki awake. I had kissed her and told her I wasn't tired, then went to her old room, now our study and paced. Eventually falling asleep in the chair by the fireplace, I slept fitfully. But as I listened at Gerry's door, the voices grew distinct.

"...shouldn't have stayed over. I should go before anyone wakes." A female voice I had difficulty placing said.

"Isn't that usually the man's line?" Gerry replied.

There was a pause. "I'm glad you came back," the female voice said. "I missed you. But Gerry, we can't do this. I can't do this. I've lied by omission because you asked me to. You know how it made me feel every time I heard about you? Every time I walked in, and they were talking about where could you be?"

"And I told you why," Gerry said.

"Yes, I know, but... you have no idea how it was. What it was like. I know why you wanted to be alone, but over a year? Gerry, you have to admit, it's been too long."

"I only just found him, Brit, how could I come back before my task was done?"

Britney? I shook off my surprise. What on earth was she doing in Gerry's room?

"I do know, and I understand. But to treat your family that way? I know you're angry, you have every right to be. But sometimes I wonder. Did I do the right thing? You came back even angrier than when you left. Don't make me regret my choice."

"I don't mean to. I wasn't planning on being angry. I was going to grovel at everyone's feet and beg forgiveness for putting them all through that, but then Ross called me that–"

"What? Bastard? You know what he meant. Just because you're sensitive to that word, doesn't make it all right for you to act like a... a..."

"Bastard?"

"Exactly."

"I know, but it doesn't help. I knew what he meant. Dammit we used to call each other that all the time and it never made a speck of difference to me but now... I see him everywhere, Brit. I see the man who hurt my mother, who abandoned his sons, and one I will never have the satisfaction of destroying."

"I know." There was silence for a moment, and I held my breath. "But, you know what could help? Your family. Your friends."

"You?"

"No, Ger, you know I can't. It was a onetime thing," she answered. "I shouldn't have let you talk me into staying last night. I can't. No one knows about us. And I want it to stay that way."

"Are you ashamed of me?"

"What?" she gasped. "No! I... no, Gerry. I cared very deeply for you. Even before you saved me, I cared. But things have changed. You've been gone for over a year."

There was a pause. "Are you seeing someone?"

"So what if I was," she said.

"Not my place, got it."

"No, it's not. But," she sighed, "there's not been anyone since you. You were my first, remember?"

"I do," he answered softly. There was a shuffle, and I wasn't sure if Gerry was getting out of bed, but my mind was whirling with the revelation. All that time, Britney knew where he was, knew what he was doing. And she lied to us. A lie of omission is still a lie in my book. Shaking my head to clear it, I listened again. "...but you know why I did what I did. In fact, it was you who encouraged me, if you recall."

"I told you to follow your gut. But I was hoping you would be back. You stopped texting me months ago. What was I supposed to think?"

"I'm sorry," he grunted, familiar as I was with my best

friend, I knew he had thrust his fingers through his hair and turned away. "I had just had my first solid lead on where he might be, and I ignored all things other than that. And you just happen to be one of the casualties."

"Oh, I just happened to be, huh?" Britney answered sarcastically. "Look, I need to go. I shouldn't have stayed this long. I'm sure people will be getting up soon and I would really rather not cause a scandal."

"Scandal?" his voice held a teasing lilt. "Are we in the eighteenth century, Miss Boyle? Would there be a scandal?"

"Talk," she amended. "I don't want anyone to talk. I've always been the girl who was looked at as a child."

"You're far from a child."

"I know that."

"So do I."

"Yes, I know, Ger, but you know what I'm talking about."

"I do," he sighed. "Your secret scandalous nature is safe with me."

There was a pause. "Talk to Ross. He really was beside himself with worry. He looked for you everywhere. He would hate me if he found out."

"I will. He will understand."

No, I bloody well do not, I swore.

"Brit," Gerry called. "I've always cared about you. You know that?"

"I do," she answered. "I've always cared about you too. I'm glad you're home."

I stood tall. Part of me thought about running down the hall and hiding in an alcove I knew was there, but the other part of me wanted them to know I overheard. And that was the part that won out. Britney opened the door and froze.

"Shit," she breathed. "How much have you heard?"

"Enough," I stated. "I want answers. Now."

"And I'll give them to you," Gerard said from inside the room. "Come inside, Ross. Brit, get back to your room. I'll handle this."

Britney glanced at Gerry and then back at me. "I'm sorry." She whispered, then rushed down the hall to her room. I stepped into Gerry's room taking in the sight of the unmade bed, the fire in the gas fireplace, and the duffle bag on the corner chair.

Gerry turned to pull on a pair of jeans over his black briefs and slipped on a sweater. I stayed rigid by the door waiting. Finally, Gerry looked over at me.

"Is coffee allowed first or do you want to get on with railing at me?"

"Don't be a smart arse," I spat. "You disappeared for over a year. Why didn't you at least call me?"

"I assume you heard our conversation. You know why."

"About that. Since when? You and Brit? She's lied to me. To us."

"She didn't lie to anyone. She kept my secret. I asked her. She did it for me. If you're angry at anyone, be angry at me."

"Oh I am," I answered. "But she is my fiancée's best friend. You had no right to get her to lie for you."

"Look," he sighed, crossing his arms over his chest. "Can you just punch me and get it over with?"

I seriously contemplated it, but I noticed the antique desk standing behind him and didn't want to break it. But then the thought of drawing blood from a broken nose was too much a temptation. Walking over to him, I reared back and held. Gerard deserved it. He absolutely deserved it in my opinion, but he didn't react. He didn't raise his hand to stop me or protect himself. He didn't do anything. He just stood there waiting. I took a deep breath and let it out slowly. Lowering my hand, I stared at him.

"What happened to you, Gerry?"

"A lot."

"Talk to me. We used to be so close. You're a stranger to me now."

"I know," he huffed. "I'm sorry, Ross. I..." he turned from me and looked out the window. "It's been a long year."

"Talk to me," I said again.

He hesitated but eventually nodded. Turning back to me, he indicated the settee behind us. "Sit with me?"

Chapter

Six

Nikki

Ross hadn't come to bed all night. When I woke, seeing my fiancé was not by my side, I dressed and went down to the kitchen. Ross and I were comfortable making our own breakfast, but I wanted to make sure my friends and family had something, so I put on some Christmas music and placed the kettle for tea on the stove and began to brew a pot of coffee for my dad. As I opened the industrial refrigerator, I eyed the couple dozen eggs, sausage, cheese, and produce. Deciding to make my famous, in my opinion, scrambled eggs with sausage and potatoes skillet, I grabbed the potatoes from the pantry and started dicing up an onion, bell pepper, and sausage. I reveled in the mundane activity. Cooking was always something I enjoyed but hardly had time for. Early in our relationship, Ross and I would get up before dawn and cook early on a Saturday morning before Marcus arrived.

As I diced a few potatoes, I looked up through the window at the snow-covered ground. The dark sky and the cold from the day before, turned out to be a foot and a half of snow. The row of trees that cut across the property was draped in glowing white, and the ground was covered in powdery snow. Christmas was always my most favorite time of year. For many years back in America, my dad and I would go out on Black Friday and pick out our Christmas tree, putting it up in the living room while the fire danced in the fireplace, Christmas music played from the YouTube app on the TV, and hot cocoa simmered on the stove. We would then turn out all the lights apart from the fire, the twinkle lights on the tree, and the garlands, and simply enjoy each other's company. I missed those days. Not that I wasn't happy with my current circumstances, but I did miss the simplicity of life back then.

After cutting up the potatoes and putting them into the pan with some olive oil to brown, I took my coffee mug and stood back at the window. The eggs would be done far too quickly if I started them now. The sausage and potatoes needed a good thirty minutes and though I needed to watch the food cooking, I couldn't take my eyes off the grounds.

As I stared out at the snow, my mind wandered to Angus and what his traditions would have been during the holidays. Then, thinking of how many Christmases he watched, all of the years, alone, and invisible, my heart hurt.

"Happy Christmas, Angus," I said softly as I gazed out at his old, rusted water pump dusted with snow yet still visible. "Miss you. I wish I could talk to you just one more time."

Taking a sip from the coffee, the hot bitter sweetness touched my tongue, and I closed my eyes as the holiday blended flavor exploded across my tastebuds. Two more sips and I opened my eyes again, warming my hands on the ceramic reindeer mug. Movement caught my eyes out the frosted windowpanes. Looking over, I could see something large moving just beyond the line of trees, but I couldn't make out what it was. The glass was too foggy to see much in detail. But I had the distinct impression I was being watched.

"Oh, forgive me, Miss Thompson," Iain's voice jerked me out of my thoughts. I turned to Ross's assistant and smiled.

"Good morning, Iain," I said. "I hope you had a wonderful evening. Thank you for all your hard work on getting everyone here. It really means a lot to me that you took the time and effort."

"It was my pleasure, Miss," he said.

"And I'm glad you didn't leave when it was so late."

"I am thankful to have been able to stay over. I make my way home to Invergordon as soon as possible."

"Oh, my I hope the roads are cleared," I glanced toward the window again.

"I am fortunate enough to have a proper car to drive in this weather. I'll be fine. Thank you for your concern, Miss."

"Of course, and you're from the Highlands. Just like I'm from the Midwest, we learn how to drive in this."

"Indeed," he said and forced a smile. "Would you mind if I have some coffee?"

"Oh of course!" I jumped to get him a mug.

"Thank you, but you don't have to serve me, Miss Thompson."

"It's Nikki, and it's my pleasure. After everything you've done, it's the least I can do." I poured him a mug full and offered cream and sugar both of which he declined and like me, took it black. "I'm working on sausage and potatoes and am going to make some scrambled eggs. Will you join me?" I moved back to the skillet and pulled the potatoes off the heat to work on the sausage.

"I would, Miss... Nikki, but I am actually allergic to eggs. But I'll take some of that skillet, smells divine."

"Allergic? To eggs?" I questioned as he sat at the kitchen table. "That's not a usual allergy you hear about."

"Oh, I'm well aware," he chuckled. "I had a date once tell me she thought I was making it up and ordered her steak with Hollandaise sauce and had me try some."

"Oh my," my eyebrows rose. "What happened?"

"I honestly don't remember much. I went into anaphylaxis shock and woke up in hospital. Needless to say, there was no second date."

I couldn't help my laugh. "I would imagine not! Wow." Shaking my head, I broached a similar subject. "Speaking of dating, I couldn't help but notice you were talking with Britney last night. You two seemed... interested."

He sighed. "I wanted to talk to her since she arrived. I hadn't seen her before yesterday and damn is she pretty."

"She is," I affirmed. "And very sweet."

"But it was pretty clear she didn't want me after Mr. Fergus arrived. So I suppose I'm too late."

"Did she talk about him?"

"No, that's why I was wondering. I don't want to tread in some bloke's territory. Been there before and won't do it again."

"She just never mentioned him to me." I shrugged. "I wonder why."

"Because I didn't know how." Britney's voice from the doorway surprised us both.

"Brit, hey," I turned from the stove, pulling the sausage skillet off the heat and walking to my best friend. "I'm sorry, I just didn't know about you and Gerry, and I saw you and Iain talking yesterday and thought I could work my matchmaking skills." I glanced over apologetically at Iain who looked decidedly uncomfortable. I headed back to the stove and plated some potatoes and sausage for Iain.

"I know," she answered. "And truth be told..." she huffed. "I don't know the truth. Iain, I did really like our conversation and I hope maybe, if you want, we can continue it sometime?"

"Ehm," Iain started. "I don't know."

Brit looked down and nodded. "I understand."

"It's not that I don't think you're a fine lass," he went on quickly. "It's just, you and Fergus have history. I don't want to butt in."

"There is history, I won't deny it, but it's just that. History."

"Look," I started. "Why don't you exchange numbers and if one of you decides to text or call the other and that person doesn't answer, then you know. I know Iain needs to get home and with the snow, he'll drive slower than usual."

Iain and Brit locked eyes and he shrugged. "I'm game if you are."

Brit smiled sweetly at him and nodded. As they exchanged numbers, I refilled my coffee and combined the rest of the potatoes and sausage. Putting it in one of the ovens to keep warm, I turned back to the fridge and grabbed the premade biscuits. Checking the clock, it was nearly nine and Ross had promised breakfast would be ready by then. Wondering where my laird was since he was supposed to help me, I knew he must be speaking with Gerard, it was the only thing important enough to miss our breakfast date.

I pulled out the eggs and set the carton down next to the chopped produce I had fixed earlier. Once the biscuits were in the main oven, I found the olive oil and another sauté pan, humming along to *Silent Night* playing from my music streaming app on my phone. The oil just the right temperature, I tossed in the onions, bell pepper, garlic, and kept a small amount separate adding a jalapeño for dad. I reveled in the smokey garlicy smells rising in the kitchen.

After a moment, I turned back to crack the eggs and whisk them together when I saw Iain smile at Brit and look over at me.

"Miss Thompson, thanks so much for the coffee and friendly chat. I'll be off if you think Laird Sutherland doesn't need me."

"I'm sure he doesn't. You sure I can't make you a plate for the road?"

"Thank you but that was plenty and delicious. I really should get going. Next time though."

"I'll hold you to that. And please give your mother our compliments and be sure to give her the weekend stay voucher. From what you told me, she could do with some pampering looking after your seven nieces and nephews."

"I will be sure to, Miss Thompson. And Happy Christmas to you and his lairdship."

"Happy Christmas, Iain! Safe travels!" I beamed as he headed out of the kitchen. I loved the idea of family coming home for Christmas.

Brit and I stayed in silence for a little while, apart from the music through the Bluetooth speaker, the occasional groan of the castle as the wind blew against the old stone outside, and the hiss of the radiators kicking on. I didn't want to push but I also wanted answers. Whipping a dozen and half of eggs, in the large bowl, I seasoned the mixture and poured it over the nicely browned garlic and translucent onions. The bubbling and gurgling sounds were satisfying. I turned the burner down to medium low and started scraping the sides as my dad had taught me.

"He was my first." The words hung between us in the kitchen as Brit announced what exactly her relationship was to my fiancé's cousin.

"It's none of my business, Britney," I began. "But I would like to hear the story. I consider you and Jess my best friends. I would have hoped you would have been able to talk to me about this."

"I know. And I did try, in my way. A few months ago."

I remembered the times she mentioned a guy she was interested in, but I had just gotten my tour schedule and didn't have much time to talk to her.

"The guy you talked about was Gerry?"

She nodded. Pausing for a long moment, she finally stood, grabbed Iain's mug, and headed to the sink. Washing and drying the snowman shaped cup, she went to the coffee pot and poured a cup. Finally, when she sat down, she began.

Chapter Seven

Britney

Last February

I should never have come. I knew it wasn't going to be fun for me seeing my sister all gaga over her new boyfriend. The tan line from her engagement ring had barely faded and she was on to the next notch. All right, that was unfair, but it was hardly kosher. And it had absolutely nothing to do with the fact that I had liked Graeme Fergus first. Nope, absolutely nothing. I rolled my eyes.

I made the mistake of telling her I thought he was cute and really sweet. He was the only one who paid any attention to me. We used to talk, and I thought... man, I was stupid, I thought I could win him. But enter Jess. She came over to where we were talking one day and that was the last time Graeme Fergus looked at me. It hurt.

But I flew over to Scotland to be with Nikki on her birthday and there they stood beside Ross and Nikki. Graeme's arm over Jess's shoulders looking like a young happy couple. I ached for that. I wanted it so badly. I never understood why Jess competed with me. I was nothing special. Hardly anything to look at, young and inexperienced to boot. But whatever Jessica Boyle wanted, she got, no matter who she hurt to get it. It wasn't the first time I had been "out Jessed". Grabbing another glass of champagne from the open bar, I wandered over near the group of four.

"You sure you're wanting to do this, mate?" Graeme was speaking to Ross. "Minivan, car seat, married man paunch?"

"One, I'll never have a minivan," Ross started. "Two, does it bloody look like I'm going to have a paunch now or ever?" Lifting his sweater, he revealed his abs. Nikki was practically salivating. I blushed. Ross was hot, but it wasn't my place to look. "Three," he lowered his sweater and tugged Nikki closer to him. "I cannae think of anything I want more than a car seat in the back of my Range Rover."

"Nothing, baby?" Nikki questioned suggestively.

From her wiggling eyebrows and Ross's short laugh, I could tell a car seat wasn't the only thing on their minds when they thought of Ross's back seat.

"But children, though wanted, are far into the future," Ross said. "Nikki's career is taking off and I need to get through the media shitestorm that's about to happen when I go public."

Their conversation carried on, but I strolled along the room looking at the books that lined the walls. A good story never let me down. I happened to glance over at the wrong moment to see Graeme and Jess kiss. I decided it was time for a little pity party. Yes, I said it. Everyone needs one every now and then and it was time.

I had to leave the castle. Pulling on my coat and boots as it was about to dip below freezing that night, I hurried out the back door and walked around the grounds. Heading through the row of trees into the thicker part of the forest, the night was waning fast. And soon, to my horror, I was lost. The wind picked up and the first of the snowflakes were starting to fall around me. I shivered.

"Don't panic. Look for light." There was no light. And I was starting to panic. The wind bit and my entire body hurt and ached. I needed to find shelter. There were already a couple inches of snow on the ground. My boots were decorative not practical, and soon my socks and toes were completely wet and cold.

"Don't panic."

I kept walking but soon realized I was walking in a large circle. There was a very distinctive gnarled tree that I had passed before. More snow, more wind, more colder temperatures. I soon couldn't feel my face and my fingers and toes were numb.

"Sssssstupid, ssssssstupid idddea, Bbbbbritney," I stuttered. The snow covered my feet to my ankles and kept coming down fast. My vision was starting to blur, and my feet faltered. I landed face first into a soft pile of feathery light snow and everything went black.

I slowly woke. I was warm. Hot actually. But it was so nice. I took a deep breath, my body aching. Slowly opening my eyes, I was inside a small single room cabin. A roaring fire blazed in the hearth beside me, and I was laying in a heavy wooden bed covered in what felt like a thousand blankets. I reveled in the ability to wiggle my toes and lifted the blankets. Immediately, I screeched and lowered them back to my chest.

I was naked.

My gaze pinballed around the room looking for my clothes. My jeans and sweater, shoes and socks, were laid out before the fire and my... I gulped, underthings were drying on the grate. I tried to sit up, but my body protested. Falling back down to the bed, I tried not to panic but soon I heard the crunch of boots on snow and the door opened. I immediately closed my eyes and pretended to be asleep but kept one eye slightly open to make sure whoever it was would not attack me. All I could see was a large person, tall, well built, muscular under their layers of black coat, scarf, hat, gloves, boots, jeans that looked insulated, and a beanie. He carried split wood in a bundle under one arm and a pail filled with snow in another. He stamped his boots, kicking off the snow that crusted the leather. He then pulled them off and walked over to the fire. Setting the bundle of wood on top of the pile, I watched out of my slightly closed eye as he shook out of his scarf and coat. He then pulled off his beanie and set his outerwear on the grate next to my things, slinging the coat over a coat hanger next to the hearth. His back was to me as he pulled off his sweater and undershirt.

I gulped as so much of his body was revealed. Still only seeing his back, his skin looked smooth with a couple moles darkening his lower and mid back and some freckles that popped against his shoulders. A sleeve tattoo marked his left arm His blonde hair was trimmed close at the back and sides but remained long up top. He pushed a hand through his blonde locks and even though it was freezing cold, his hair looked sweaty and messy.

He turned to the massive and intricately carved wardrobe in the corner at the foot of the bed. Opening the doors he pulled out a brown sweater and tugged it on. He then removed his jeans. I captured my gasp as his briefs were the only thing preventing me from seeing his backside. Though I did admit, it was a fine-looking backside, I looked away. I sensed movement and slowly looked back to the man. He was before the fire again but this time, I saw a dog with him. No, not a dog, a wolf, and it was staring at me. I whimpered and immediately clamped my lips shut.

"Balach," a soft Scottish voice commanded. "Come." The wolf obeyed and padded over to him. Laying on the floor before the fire, the wolf watched with frighteningly intelligent blue eyes.

"You can open your eyes now," the voice continued. "Or are you going to pretend you're asleep for the rest of the evening?" He turned to me, and I gasped.

Opening my eyes to see him fully, "Gerard?" I questioned.

Chapter Eight

Nikki

Present Day

"So you stayed with him? All that time?" I asked Britney when she finished her story.

"It was only a week," she answered shrugging. "We got close. It was nice, you know? Someone that was actually mine."

I looked down. "I'm sorry," I said. "I know what you've gone through and did nothing. I've seen Jess do that to you. I'm sorry you felt like you had to leave. I'm just glad you're okay."

"Me too. He saved my life. I fell in love with him."

"Then why did he leave?"

"Because I told him to. He was so distraught over learning about his conception. He was so depressed and wanted to do some sort of damage. I mentioned perhaps if he found his father, he would be able to get the sort of closure he needs. We... made love the last day he was there. It was... amazing and wonderful, and I wouldn't change a single thing. But it's over. We both agreed that when he left it was over. I wouldn't be pining for him, and I haven't been, it just... no other guy has come close to measuring up to him. Or Balach."

"The wolf?" I questioned plating the eggs into one of the containers to carry to the breakfast room.

"Yeah," she grinned. "He was there off and on. He would scratch at the door some nights and Gerard would let him in. He would lay before the fire and watch us. I swear there were times when I thought he knew what we were saying. He was the sweetest thing too. I missed him. I wonder if he's okay."

"I just have one more question," I got back on the subject as I pulled the sausage skillet out of the oven to pour into the carry container. "Why didn't you tell us? At least tell me where he was or that he was safe? Ross was worried sick."

"I know, and I felt horrible about that. But Gerry asked me not to. He begged me to let him be. He swore he would come back as soon as he found his father. He told me last night that he only just got the solid lead on his father a month or so ago."

"Last night? You stayed over with him?" I asked.

She looked away. "I went to check on him and make sure he was okay. He invited me in, and we talked. After a while, I kissed him to welcome him back and one thing led to another. I just came from his room. Ross knows. He was listening at the door."

My stomach dropped. Ross knew. He wouldn't be happy about all this. I needed to find him.

"Look, why don't you help me get everything into the

52

breakfast room and I'll go talk to him."

"Okay," she answered. "Just please, don't let him kick me or Gerry out. We honestly didn't mean to hurt him or lie to him. I was keeping Gerry's secret."

"I would never allow him to kick you out and he never would. It's okay, Brit. Really. I'm just so sorry you ever felt alone while I was there. But I know what it's like to be lonely. Promise me, you'll say something next time and not just run off?"

"I promise," Britney smiled.

I pulled the biscuits out of the oven and grinned, proud of myself that they didn't burn. Together, we carried the tea kettle, eggs, biscuits, and potatoes to the breakfast room. Chad, Frank, James, and Jenn were already seated when we arrived. They greeted us happily and Chad immediately asked for details.

"Spill the tea, babe," he ordered as he buttered a biscuit and slathered jam over the flakey bread.

"Not much to tell," I answered.

"Don't play coy, honey, it's not a good look."

I laughed at him. "It's not my story to tell, Chad. Besides, even if it was, I wouldn't want my dirty laundry aired in the open."

"Fine," he huffed. "I'll come to your room later, but I expect gossip."

"And you'll get it, promise."

He winked and then moaned as he bit into the biscuit.

"Careful with those sounds you're making, babe," Frank deadpanned. Chad grinned but continued to eat as everyone busted out laughing.

Something caught my eye and I looked out the windowed doors of the breakfast room that led to the back of the castle, the row of trees, and Angus's pump. There, staring at me, standing just at the hedgerow, stood a large grey wolf.

"What on earth–" I started.

"They're here," Brit cut me off and I looked over to see Ross, Graeme, and Gerard walk in. Ross looked tense but he smiled slightly when he saw me. The other two glanced around the room.

"Sorry about last night, everyone," Gerard said. "I hope it's all right if I stay?"

"All right with me, handsome, but I expect answers," Chad replied pulling out the empty chair next to him.

"Chadwick," Frank grunted.

"Hush, husband of mine," Chad replied. "Now, tell me everything."

Gerard looked lost as Chad lifted his teacup and eyed him over the rim.

Ross sat beside me, a plate of food in front of him.

"All right?" I asked.

"Far from it, but better," he replied.

"Did you get your answers?"

Ross sighed. "Not the answers I was wanting, but yes."

"What answers were you wanting?"

"I honestly don't know. But I'm just glad to have him back."

"I know you are." I took his hand and squeezed. "If I had known that Brit knew..."

"Gerard fell on his sword for her. Claimed it was his idea and she was just following what he asked."

"You don't believe that?" I questioned softly, not wanting to interrupt the other conversations.

"I... I don't know. She's your best friend. She knew

firsthand how worried I was, and she didn't say anything?"

"She and I talked as I cooked breakfast."

"Sorry by the way for skipping out on helping you," he kissed my hand. "This looks delicious."

"Thank you and no worries," I smiled. "I knew you were probably talking to him. But she told me everything and I truly believe she did what she did thinking it would help him. She basically talked him off a ledge. It was her idea to channel his emotions."

"I know," he answered. "I honestly don't want to talk about it anymore. He's back where he belongs. That's all that matters."

"Agreed," I replied. Then after a moment, I went on. "I'm planning on going into the village later today. I don't have anything for Chad or Jess for Christmas, and I want to make sure they have a wonderful Christmas. It'll be the first holiday we're all together."

"Sure, yeah, sounds great. Do you want me to come with you?"

"If you want," I answered. "I already have your Christmas present." My voice dropped to what I hoped was a seductive tone.

"Oh?" he matched my timbre. "If it's anything like your Ugly Christmas Sweater surprise then I'm sure to love it."

"I don't think you'll be disappointed."

"I like the sound of that," he answered. "I think I can safely promise a not so silent night." Winking, he turned back to his food but when he lifted a fork full of sausage potatoes, he locked eyes with me and licked it off the utensil.

"Dear god," Chad's voice broke my thoughts. Looking over at him, he was watching us and took the saucer of his teacup to fan himself. Frank rolled his eyes and let out a long-suffering sigh.

The door opened and dad, Jackie, Jess, and Marilyn walked in. Gerard got up from the table and instantly went to his mother. Engulfing her in a hug, he held her tightly as she clutched his back.

"Oh my sweet boy." She wept.

"I'm so sorry, mum," he replied softly. "You know I love you, aye? I was angry."

"I know, love," she answered.

"I could never blame you for something he did."

"You don't hate me?"

"Hate you?" He breathed. "My god, mum everything you do for me? For us? How could you think I hate you? Never. You hear me?" he pulled back to look in her eyes. "And you have nothing to be ashamed of. It was his sin and I hope he's burning in hell for it."

"Gerry," Graeme cautioned.

"Sorry, but after what I found out? I have no filter when it comes to him."

"What did you find out?" Brit asked.

"You don't want to know."

"I do," Chad piped up.

Gerard sighed. "You're not the only one he did that to, okay? I... met our kid brother."

"What?" we all questioned.

"Aye, his last... whatever you want to call it, girlfriend seems too nice of a word, had a kid but didn't remember getting pregnant after drinking too much at a club one night. Ollie is seven."

"Oh my god," Marilyn cried. "That poor woman."

"When were you going to tell me this?" Graeme asked.

"Today, but I didn't think it was an appropriate conversation to have over the breakfast table," Gerry said.

"Do they need help?" Marilyn asked.

"No, one thing he did right was take care of them when he died." Gerard walked with his mother back to the breakfast table.

"I just can't believe it," Marilyn sat down almost in a daze.

"We can talk more about it later," Gerard said and went to get a plate for his mother.

"Are you all right, Mari?" Jackie asked.

"Honestly, no," she replied. "But I'm sure it won't take me long. The man has been out of my life for thirty plus years. I'm just sorry for the woman."

Gerard placed a plate in front of his mother. "Can we talk about something else?"

"Sure," Graeme said. "What's this I hear about you sleeping with Britney?"

Britney sputtered in her tea and nearly choked.

"I was hoping we could decorate the tree today," I offered, changing the subject.

"That would be fun," Jackie replied playing into my conversation.

"A little caroling, maybe a Christmas movie?" I said.

"Ooh, ooh, *The Holiday?* Because who doesn't love some Jude Law?" Chad licked his lips.

"I was thinking *Die Hard*," Frank answered.

"Babe, for the last time *Die Hard* is *not* a Christmas movie."

"Yes it is," all the men said at the same time.

Chad stared at each in turn. "Dear god, all this machismo

is suffocating," he grimaced.

"I was thinking *White Christmas,*" I piped up.

"Who can say no to a classic?" Ross replied.

"And then we can watch *Die Hard?*" Dad asked.

"Once Chad and I leave to go shopping you all can watch Hans Gruber fall off the Nakatomi building to your heart's content," I said.

Everyone stared at me, and I knew my bluff had been called out.

"Okay fine," I surrendered. "So, I've seen it... A few times." Still, everyone was silent. "Fine, I watched it nearly every week while writing *Secret Revenge.*"

"So..." Ross drew out. "Inquiring minds want to know, love. And your answer could greatly affect our relationship status," Ross teased. "Do you believe *Die Hard* is a Christmas movie?"

My immediate answer was *no* but... "If you think it is, baby then I agree. It does happen on Christmas Eve."

"Thank you," Frank replied.

"That's my girl." Dad winked.

"Traitor," Chad grumbled.

"*But* that does not mean I'm going to watch it *for* Christmas. Enjoy, boys. Chad? Shopping?"

"You said the magic word. All is forgiven." He held his hand out toward Frank who sighed and pulled out his wallet.

Handing him a credit card, he pulled it back and gave his husband a stern look. "Keep it under a thousand, Chadwick."

"No promises, handsome," Chad kissed Frank's cheek and looked over at me. "Ready, babe?"

Laughing, I piled the utensils on my plate and looked around the table. "Anyone for shopping?"

Chapter Nine

Waking earlier than my usual time, I glanced over at Ross who was still asleep, laying on his stomach, one arm slung protectively across my abdomen. Smiling at his sleeping face, I kissed his forehead and wiggled out of bed. Looking out the window, the sun was shining on the white snow, but the path had been cleared by a local village boy and I was itching for a good run. It had been too long.

Padding over to the wardrobe, I opened the drawers and searched for my fleece lined leggings, zip up hoodie, and earmuffs. Dressing and pulling on my wooly socks and infinity scarf, I was ready for a run. Whispering to Ross, "I'm going for a run," I beamed when he hummed, nodded, and pulled my pillow closer to him.

Leaving our room, making sure to not let the door shut loudly, I hurried down the steps to the back door. The first time I had been at the castle hotel's off season when we had no guests, or very few, was eerie. Now, it was a time I anticipated and reveled in. The breakfast room was silent as I headed toward the library bar and out the back. Knowing Ross would help me with breakfast, I set my timer for an hour, stretched, and opened the door. The cold hit me and stole my breath. Perhaps it would be better if I stayed inside. I could go down to the workout room and run on the treadmill. But the allure of fresh air and sunshine won out.

Pushing off the last step, I started running at a slow jog letting my muscles get acquainted with running again and warm up. I steadied my breathing to prepare for the cold and never felt more alive. After a while at my steady clip, I picked up the pace and soon was back to my usual speed.

It was nearly forty minutes later when I pulled up and bent at the waist to get a good breath in. My nose and cheeks were red from wind and cold burn, but my body was limber and felt oh so good. Looking around to see where I was, I would know the spot blindfolded. The castle loomed before me in all its beauty, but to my left stood Angus's pump.

Walking over to it, I kissed my gloved fingers and pressed them to the top. The pump had served as his unconsecrated burial plot marker. When we were searching for the Highland Pride together, I would meet him standing just beside it. When we had found the Pride and he had passed over, I would come out and lay flowers or if I was missing him particularly much, I would talk to him. That day was a mixture of feelings.

"Oh, Angus," I breathed. "I do miss you. I wish more than anything to be able to talk to you again. Ross could use your wisdom and I just really miss our talks. I guess with the holidays approaching, I keep thinking of you, all those years, alone here. All those Christmases passing by and you unable to speak with anyone. How sad it must have been. I'm so sorry for it. Is there any way you could give me a sign? Just something for me to know you're all right?"

I knew how strange it was. Me wishing to speak with a ghost. But he wasn't just any ghost. He was my ghost.

With another sigh, I kissed my fingers again and pressed them to the pump. "Love you always, Angus. Happy Christmas."

I turned to go when I heard a soft whimper. I looked and nearly stumbled back. The wolf. The same one I had seen watching me the previous morning, appeared at the break of the hedgerow. He was watching me again. His blue eyes were frighteningly intelligent. Odd, I never knew wolves had blue eyes. But he padded softly through the snow toward me. I took a step back. Bile rose in my throat knowing I would never make it back to the castle before he attacked. I merely watched him, warily.

Britney's story came back to me. Was this Gerard's wolf?

"Balach?" I questioned.

Balach moved toward the pump, not toward me. I tilted my head curious. I felt no threat. Then, to my surprise, he nuzzled the old pump. He never dropped my gaze, but he nuzzled the old water pump with his head. My eyes narrowed as I watched. He kept his gaze on me as he did it again.

Blue eyes. Old pump. Waiting for me. "Angus?" I breathed.

The wolf stopped and pulled up to his full height but dipped his head in affirmation.

"What?" I couldn't seem to get my breath. The wolf stared at me as I gasped for air unable to fill my lungs. "An... Angus." I reached out for him as my world went dark and I fell into the snow.

Ross

I woke clutching Nikki's pillow. I had a vague recollection of my future wife telling me she was going for a run. Taking a deep breath, I inhaled her scent and smiled. I loved that perfume. I had bought it for her birthday and loved how it smelled on her. My eyes adjusted to the light streaming in from the window near the bed. It was a sunny morning, but I could feel how cold it was, though the radiator kicked on just as I sat up.

Slipping out of the sheets, I headed to the bathroom, then dressed. It was the Winter Solstice today, a day I always enjoyed celebrating as part of my Celtic heritage. We didn't do much but performed some traditions like going out in search of mistletoe and if found, cutting a piece, and hanging it over our doorway. It was a symbol of life in the coldness of winter. I missed last year's event by being in Edinburgh finishing up a talk but that year, I was certain would be a wonderful time. But first, I needed to find my fiancée.

Grabbing my phone, I sent her a text.

Ross: Good morning, beautiful. Finished your run? I miss you already.

It was only eight in the morning, but I had no idea when she had gotten up. Heading downstairs, I met Chad and Frank in the breakfast room laying out some biscuits and gravy, along with some sort of breakfast casserole.

"Damn, lads, smells amazing," I smiled.

They looked over and greeted me with a beaming "good morning".

"Where's our girl?" Chad asked. "Wear her out last night, Sutherland?"

"Ha," I chuckled. "The opposite in fact. She left hours before I got up. Went for a run. Haven't seen her, have you?"

"Not here," Frank answered. "Or in the kitchen. Chad and I were up early and thought we'd surprise everyone with breakfast."

"It looks amazing. Thank you so much. I'm going to do a quick check and see if I can find her then I'll join you," I said.

"Sounds good," Chad got a plate and began filling it with food.

I made my way to the gym. She wasn't there, it was cold and dark. Then, I headed to the library bar. It was empty apart from Marilyn. She looked up when I came in.

"Good morning, dear," she smiled tiredly.

"Morning, Marilyn," I answered. "You haven't seen Nikki, have you?"

"No, should I have?" she questioned.

"She just left early for a run, and I haven't seen her yet. She must be taking a long one. Not to worry."

"All right."

"Chad and Frank have made breakfast if you're hungry."

"Ooh, it smells amazing. I got caught up in writing. I'll be there in a moment."

"No rush," I smiled at her but the knots in my stomach were churning. I needed to find her. I had a horrible feeling. And the last time I had that feeling... it didn't bear thinking.

Hurrying up to her old room which we converted into a study for us both, I knocked and opened the door only to find it empty. As I walked back down the hallway, Gerard exited his room and looked over at me.

"What's wrong?" he asked. I had to admit, it was nice to have my best friend back.

"I can't find Nikki."

"How long?"

"A few hours. I slept in and she went for a run."

"Well, then why are you so worried?"

"Because of the last time she went missing. I don't know. She's been... distant recently. Missing Angus and the excitement of adventure. I don't know." I hadn't voiced my insecurities to anyone over the last few months, but it was different with Gerard. He was always the quiet, levelheaded one of the three of us.

"Hmm," he sighed. "She seemed all right yesterday. If she's just gone for a run, she'll be back."

"And if she's not?"

"Have you tried calling her?"

"I texted," I explained. "It's really cold out there too. I don't want her to have hurt herself and not be able to make it back."

"Do you know her jog route?"

"Usually, aye."

"Then let's go," he offered and went back into his room to grab his coat and scarf.

I breathed a sigh of relief when he fell into step with me. *Where are you, Nikki?*

Chapter Ten

Nikki

I woke with a splitting headache. Lying on my back in the snow, I shivered and sat up. My body and head protested the movement. I reached out to hold onto the pump to help me stand but my hand met air. Looking over, there was no pump.

Odd, I thought as I checked the area around me. *Where is Angus's pump?*

Unable to think any more on it and only wanting to get back to the castle and have a fresh cup of coffee to warm me up and stand before the fireplace with Ross, I stood. Weaving, I planted my feet in the foot and a half of snow to brace my body. Once the cloudiness had vanished and the bile had retreated in my mouth, I looked around. The castle loomed and I made my way toward the back entrance.

Before I made it out of the row of trees and onto the snow-covered gravel walkway, a man on a horse rounded the bend to my right. Seeing me, he let out a shout and kicked his horse into gear. I stood frozen as the stranger galloped in my direction, snow flying behind him. He pulled up on the horse at the last minute and sliced his claymore through the air to come to a rest under my chin.

"Who are you?" he demanded. His southern Scottish accent was not as heavy as Ross's highlander.

"What?" I questioned.

"I asked you a question, woman, if indeed a woman ye are," he ordered. "Who are you?"

"Who are you is more the question I'm interested in. My fiancé and I own this castle. What the hell do you think you're doing waving that thing around?" I stepped back so his sword fell away from my neck.

His face grew red with rage as he jumped down from his horse.

"You speak lies, wench," he went on. "MacCulloch Castle is under the ownership of the Undersheriff."

"Undersheriff?" I questioned. "What is going on here? Did Ross hire you? Iain? What is going on?"

"You dare speak the name of the enemy of the crown?" He took a menacing step forward.

"Okay, buddy. Well done, yep, good job. Really had me going there for a bit. Now, where is Ross? What is going on here?"

"Again?" he spat. "There is no Ross here. Enemies of the crown are not welcome here."

"Enemies of the crown? What is this? Some sort of reenactment? What crown?"

"The Crown of King George of England and Scotland."

I stared at him. He was serious and I laughed. "Oh okay," I mocked. "Sure, Good ole King Georgie. Well, I don't see him. In fact, no one has seen him for three hundred years! So how about you drop the act, arsehole and get the hell away from me."

"Why you little," I knew the derogatory Scottish term he nearly called me, but he didn't get a chance. As he grabbed my arm, hard, and tugged me toward him, another voice rang out over the stillness.

"What is going on here?" The voice demanded.

We both froze. He yanked me around and we both faced a man barreling down from the back entrance of the castle. My jaw dropped and my heart soared.

"Angus!" I screamed.

He looked at me and his steps faltered before he righted himself and stared at me wide eyed. I shook off the man's hand and raced to him.

"Angus!" I screamed again and threw my arms around him. He was real. He was here. Real flesh and blood here. "I've missed you so much. Oh my god!"

I took a deep breath and smelled him.

Wait.

He actually had a smell.

Pine and snowfall. Exactly what I expected him to smell like, but my Angus didn't have a scent. And he was... warm. Angus always felt ice cold and every time we touched, I felt a sort of electricity. He was here, he was breathing and... a heartbeat? What was going on? I didn't care. I clutched him even closer as tears gathered in my eyes.

"I missed you so much! How are you here?" I questioned.

Then, as if he was electrocuted, Angus jerked back, his hands came down on my arms and he pushed me back harshly. I looked up into his blue eyes, but instead of the sweetness I always saw reflected there, ferocity met me. He embodied his nickname of Fearsome MacPherson.

"Who are you?" he demanded. "What are you?"

"Angus?" I looked at him confused. "It's me. Nikki."

"I know no one by that name," he spat. "What is this? Witchcraft? Why do you look like my late wife?"

"Angus, what are you talking about?"

"She spoke about Ross, my lord," the man who grabbed me earlier came up behind me.

"What do you ken about Ross?" Angus demanded.

"Ross? You know Ross. He's my fiancé," I answered.

Angus looked up to the man behind me then down at me again and eyed my clothing. "Ross allows his woman to dress like a man?"

"What? These are my workout clothes. You've seen me in them before."

"I most certainly hae no'. I've ne'er seen ye before in my life. Your resemblance to my late wife is uncanny but I hae ne'er seen you before. However, if you are indeed Ross's fiancée, then you are of value to us. You're going to come with me."

He yanked on my arm, pulling me toward the castle. I didn't know what was going on. Angus was Angus but not my Angus. Kicking open the door, Angus tugged me inside and I looked around. This wasn't right. This wasn't my home. Everything looked... different. It was more rustic, less modern, more… ancient.

"Angus, what is going on? What happened to the castle? Where are we going? What's happening?" I fired my questions at him as we trudged through room after room.

"Angus," a female voice said as we crossed the main entryway.

He stopped and we turned, he bowed slightly to the woman. "My lady wife."

My eyes grew wide as I stared at the woman stepping off the last step of the main staircase. Her deep blue gown hugged her curves, but it was her raven hair I recognized.

"Elizabeth?" I breathed.

Her shrewd eyes flashed to me, and I felt thoroughly judged. "And who is this poor kitten?" she questioned. "One of your women, Angus? Oh dear, she looks quite done in."

"She is Ross's fiancée," Angus answered.

Her eyes flared. "Ross? You mean the laird his majesty is searching for?"

"The same," Angus replied.

"Well well well," she grinned. "How quaint. And where is your fiancé now, little one?"

"You bitch!" I screeched. "Where's your stepbrother? Haven't slept with him in a couple days?"

"You dare insult my lady wife?" Angus demanded shaking my arm.

"Ow, Angus, you're hurting me!" I cried.

"I'll do more than that," he spat. "Into the dungeon with you." Tugging me away and pushing me toward a hidden door, Elizabeth's tinkling laughter followed us.

"Angus, please," I begged when his incessant pushing got us down into the place we used as a wine cellar. But there wasn't a bottle in sight. Instead, an Iron Maiden, rack, whips, chains, and branding irons, met my eyes. "Angus?" I was starting to get scared.

"You'll be imprisoned here until Ross calls for you. And as far as your similarity to my late wife, devilry will not be tolerated in Scotland. Not under King George." He opened a cell door and tossed me inside. "Think on that verra closely."

"Angus, I know you're still working for the resistance. You are still loyal to the Bonnie Prince."

"Lies!" Angus shouted and I quaked. "I'll have no more lies nor insults from you."

"Angus, please!" I yelled as he turned toward the stairs. He wasn't listening to me. As insane as it sounded, I must have been sent back to his time. Time travel wasn't possible and yet here I was. I had to do something that caught his attention. And the best thing I had in my arsenal was something near to his heart. "Niall, I know Niall."

Angus froze on the third step. There was a long pause before he slowly turned toward me. "What do you ken of my brother?"

Here goes nothing. I thought. "I know he's buried in your family's crypt on your land up north. I know you hid the thistle key to open the tomb in the privy to make sure the English did not rob their resting places. I know you encased the lock in clay and pressed your family's crest on it. And I know your wife left your bed on your wedding night, but you asked Malcolm Brodie to lie for you."

"Witch," he spat.

"No, you told me all of this. You showed it to me."

"I did no such thing. No one knows about that. Who have

you told?" he demanded.

"No one," I lied about that since there were others, but it wasn't a lie as I had told no one in his time about it.

"I don't believe you."

"No one, I swear."

"Then how..."

"I don't know what happened. One moment I am going for a jog around the castle and the next I met a wolf and now I'm here."

Angus visibly stiffened. "A wolf?" he questioned.

"I swear to you, Angus. I don't know what is going on. Help me. Please."

He was silent for a long moment. Then, "I have no time for your falsity. Wolves have been extinct in Scotland for over a hundred years. You think me a simpleton?"

"I'm not lying to you!"

"You will stay here and think on your lies. I will send a missive to Ross lands letting him know where you are and the price for your head... and the price for the rest of you."

With that, he shuffled up the stone steps. The dark, dank room was flooded with light when he opened the door. "Angus!" I screamed as the door slammed shut, bathing me in darkness and fear.

Chapter Eleven

Angus

A wolf? On the solstice? Could it be? Nay, of course no'. The lass was a witch. How she looked so like my Riona... I shook my head.

She does look like me, love. I heard my late wife's voice in my head. I always heard her when hard decisions had to be made. *But perhaps there's a reason for that.*

Shaking my head to clear it, I stalked up the steps to my room. Hurrying to the wardrobe in the corner, I glanced at the main door as I dug for the key. How the lass in my dungeon knew I was still loyal to the Bonnie Prince, and therefore Scotland unnerved me. Had I said the wrong thing to the wrong person? I had no answers and would nae have until the night in the dungeon loosened my guest's tongue. I grabbed the key, closed the wardrobe and sat at my desk.

My door opened and I quickly hid the key to my desk drawer. Elizabeth entered. Her beauty as usual stole my breath but her cruelty was never far from her. I felt it the first time I met her.

"Is your little guest comfortable?" she asked.

"As comfortable as our dungeon can be," I answered.

"Oh good," she grinned. "I wonder…"

"What?"

"If Ross is hiding like the coward he is," she started. "Why would he allow his future wife to come here? Perhaps I should go speak with her? Woman to woman."

"I'm no' letting anyone speak to her at all until morning. A night in the dungeon will loosen her tongue. Perhaps she may even tell us where Ross is. Hae a man on standby to rush to London if we do find out."

"Well, then perhaps a little light luncheon? Join me."

"Later perhaps, love," I replied kissing her forehead. "Thank ye for the invitation. But I am going to my study. I need to see if I can send out missives to the Ross clan who still live on their land."

"It's England's land, Angus. Don't forget it. Scotland does not belong to any clan, only to England."

"Slip of the tongue," I covered.

She studied me for a long moment. "Perhaps I should have Crispin join me so I can keep him apprised of the goings on. He would be interested in knowing what is happening."

That Jackanape, I cursed silently. I'd rather tell the Butcher

Cumberland I still fought for Scotland's freedom than invite me wife's stepbrother to our home. The lass's words still echoed in my mind. Was it possible Elizabeth and Crispin...? It did nae bear thinking. Incest and adultery were sins and illegal to boot. Though they were nae blood relations.

"Arrangements are nearly complete for the Yule Soiree. Our guest list feature prominent figures. Do be sure to tame down your brogue. It is not sophisticated." With that, she swept out of the room.

With a sigh, I entered the adjoining door to the Lady of the Manor's bedchamber, connected to mine and went to her floor to ceiling mirror. Reaching up to one of the thistles decorating the corners of the mirror, I touched the round part of Scotland's national flower, it sunk in, and the mirror popped open. I had installed this secret passageway when I found the original Laird's Lug. It was the fastest and easiest way of getting to my study from my chambers and the safest way for Elizabeth and Riona, my only child named after her mother, to flee if we were ever under attack.

Padding down the steps, I reached my study. Immediately locking the door and going to the side of the room where my books lined the wall, I found my copy of Thompson's work. Allowing the book to open in the middle, I checked the binding. My confession was still there in the spine, hidden from all. I breathed a sigh of relief. But still, I wondered who this... Nikki, she said was her name, was. Placing the book back among my collection, I walked over to my desk and unlocked the side drawer. Removing the false bottom, I pulled out my bottle of Scotch and a strip of my Tartan, both illegal.

Pouring a small glass, I took it over to the fire and stared down into the flames, aimlessly caressing the faded wool. If anyone loyal to England found me with either of the two things in my hand, I would be found out and thrown in The Tower. The English stripped us, not only of our lands but of our tartans and enforced a strict English language only law. I had no' been able to speak Gaelic to anyone, apart from my daughter and Malcolm Brodie when we were alone, for years. Not being able to wish my daughter a happy Christmas in our native tongue weighed on me.

But my thoughts turned to the lass. There was something about her. Not only did she look like my Riona, but the things she knew, how she was dressed. She said a wolf appeared to her. On the Solstice. It couldn't be. She must be a witch. That was the only explanation. I took a sip of my Scotch.

Is it? I heard Riona's voice ask. *You know what a wolf means especially today. A guide to both this life and the next.*

"She says she kens me. How is that possible? How when I have ne'er met her before. And what sort of name is Nikki?" I asked the silence.

Many things are possible today of all days, my love, Riona said. *Donnae forget our culture and customs simply because you are unable to practice them.*

I took another sip and kept staring into the flames.

"What should I do?"

Try talking to her? Her teasing voice replied. *I find talking is the best way to figure out what has happened. Oh, and take her some warmer clothes, she'll freeze down there.*

With that, my wife's voice ended in my mind, and I drained my Scotch. Turning from the fire, my eyes caught the quilted blanket thrown over the settee. Huffing, I snatched it and, throwing the glass containing the remnants of the Scotch into the fire to shatter and replacing the strip of tartan, I unlocked the door and hurried down to the second entrance to the dungeon. Riona's words rang in my ears. It was the Winter Solstice and in Celtic tradition, the veil between this world and the next was thin. If this Nikki had met a wolf perhaps he guided her here. But why? And how did she ken me?

I pushed open the door and paused when I heard her weeping.

Nikki

It was so cold. I shivered. So dark. My eyes had adjusted slightly, but I almost wished they hadn't. The torture devices stared at me and loomed around the cell almost taunting me with the phantom pain they could inflict. Why was I here? How was I here? Where was *here*?

I remembered traveling with Angus in a dreamlike state when he took me through his life but the feeling of nearly drowning wasn't there. I remembered that vividly. Every time we moved from memory to memory, I felt as if I was going to drown in the darkness. This didn't feel like that. And of course, at that time, I had Angus, *my* Angus to ground me. This man was a stranger.

I had assessed my situation like my Grampa Brodie taught me, for the first twenty minutes. What did I know? Angus was there. So was Elizabeth and the castle looked different. So was it possible I had traveled through time? How did I get home? Currently, I was locked in the lowest level of the castle in a cell. Had I been able to get out of the cell, I would be able to get out of the room and eventually the castle. I knew where the secret passageways were. Perhaps I could find my way to Angus's study and force him to listen to me. But if I revealed more, would he call me a witch and burn me at the stake?

What could I reveal? That worried me too. If I revealed too much could I alter the future? I had seen enough movies to know about the butterfly effect and how life could change. If I warned Angus about his future, my past, would my future change? I had given myself a headache asking what if. All I wanted was to get back to Ross and my family and friends, curl up before the fireplace, and celebrate Christmas. Oh god, Ross. He would be so worried about me. Tears formed in my eyes and as much as I hated the idea of crying, at the moment, the situation called for a good cry. I heard a squeak of a mouse or a rat and screamed. I had to get out of there. A sob broke from my lips.

When I begged the universe to see Angus again that wasn't exactly what I had in mind. I wanted to see *my* Angus, not this complete stranger.

Oh god, he was going to die. The man I met was going to die and turn into the ghost I helped and loved in my time. Could I change that? Did I want to? How would that affect my future? Dad wouldn't come over to Scotland and meet Jackie. Jess wouldn't be with Graeme. Britney wouldn't have met Gerard and been able to talk to him. The Highland Pride wouldn't be found. And Ross and me? Would we be close?

I wouldn't lie there were times throughout our nearly yearlong engagement that I thought we might be growing apart. Our lives were so busy. We hardly had time for each other. I worried we were risking so much. We had fought a few times but when that happened we just went without talking for a few hours. But there was nothing I wouldn't give to be back in his arms.

Another sob broke from me and that time I couldn't hold it back. Curling up into a ball with my back against the cold wet stone of the cell, I wept. I didn't stop. I couldn't stop. Damn it all.

"Lass," I heard softly in the darkness. I hated that voice now. I wanted my Angus. Mine. Not this stranger. "Come now, donnae cry."

There was a flare of light as he lit a torch in the doorway and brought it over to light lamps and other torches. The room slowly lit but the fear was still heavy in the air. He could do anything he wanted to me. He had no association with me. I hoped my initial trust in Angus when I first met him wasn't misplaced and the man before still lived by his beliefs.

I tried to slow my tears as he stepped toward me. He didn't open the cell door, but he produced a quilt.

"I thought ye might be cold."

"Freezing," I hiccupped.

"Here," he offered it to me. "What in Christ's name are ye wearing?"

I didn't have an answer for that. If I truly had time traveled and it wasn't a fevered dream, he wouldn't understand *workout clothes*. But I snatched the quilt and wrapped it around my shoulders. Watching him warily as he moved a rickety old chair and sat, I stayed standing. He looked at me through the bars of my cell, studying me.

"The resemblance... forgive me, 'tis uncanny," he said.

"That is what you said when I first met you."

"When did we first meet, lass? For I donnae remember it."

What was I going to say to that? I had no answer. Angus apparently realized I was going to say nothing and sighed.

"I am trying to understand ye, lass. You need to speak with me."

"Anything I have to say, you will not understand. Hell, I don't understand."

His reaction to my curse reminded me of the first time I cursed in front of him.

"Ross allows his woman to speak in such a manner?"

"Ross Sutherland, my fiancé has no control over how I speak."

"Ross Sutherland?" he questioned.

What the hell. If I was going to die at least I was going to go out in a blaze of glory.

"Aye," I answered. "Ross Sutherland. He is the laird of the Sutherland clan."

"Nay, the Sutherland Laird is *Alexander* Sutherland, son of Alastair Sutherland who died–"

"At Culloden along with Niall," I finished.

He swallowed. "Aye. And he is only fifteen years old."

I paused. "Angus, this may sound... just please, give me an answer."

"To what question, lass?"

"What year is it?"

Angus leaned back but never dropped my gaze. "Seventeen sixty-one... why? What year are you from?"

That gave me a little encouragement. It was almost as if he was willing to listen.

"I was out for a run, it's a form of exercise, in the year two thousand and sixteen and then I woke up here."

I watched as his face gave nothing away. He still sat in his chair silent. I wasn't sure if it was a good silent or a bad. Did he believe me?

"If you're from over two hundred and fifty years in the future... how do you claim to know me?"

I licked my suddenly dry lips. "I... um... I don't know how to answer that."

"The truth would be your best option."

"The truth? Well, you seem to believe or at least are listening to me so far so... The truth is this. I live in America and am a writer, author. I came to Scotland because this place," I waved a hand around the area. "Is an author's retreat, a place where writers from all over the world can come together and work in the tranquility of nature. It's beautiful. While I was here, to me it was a little over a year ago, I met a man named Ross Sutherland. He owns MacCulloch Castle now after... um... he owns it. He and I are engaged, we've been engaged for about ten months. But while I was staying here last year, I was sent on a quest to find the Highland Pride. It's been missing since..." I couldn't give it away. "For a while."

"And who sent you on this quest?" Angus's voice was soft and intense.

I swallowed and hesitated for only a moment. "You did."

"Did you find my writings or..." he asked.

"No, not exactly. You sent me on the quest."

Angus studied me for a long moment. Then his eyes slowly slid away from me, and he stared off to the side in contemplation. He was silent for a long time, and I didn't know what I should do. But eventually he looked back up at me and his eyes held a gentleness I hadn't seen since my Angus had left.

"Who kills me?" he asked.

I didn't realize how relieved I would be for him to believe me and to figure it out. How could I possibly say *your ghost told me?*

"I don't know if I can tell you that."

"Are they in this house?"

Is Crispin Blackbourne in MacCulloch Castle at the moment? I didn't know.

"I don't know."

He took a deep breath. "Then tell me this, why were you able to see me? Do you believe in ghosts?"

"I didn't. But you said…"

"Go on."

"You told me who I was to you and that's why I can see you."

"And who are you to me?"

"Riona's line."

"My daughter?"

I nodded. "But I don't know that until you tell me."

"And when do I tell you?"

"Um… I don't know if I can tell you that either. If you know too much then my past, your future and my future could change."

Again, he was quiet, and I worried he would ask me something I couldn't answer.

"When does the Pride go missing?"

I started, then remembered, he didn't know about Niall or that the Pride was missing at all until he overheard Crispin and Elizabeth plotting… when was that? I couldn't remember. My only frame of reference was the year he died. My blood ran cold.

"What year did you say this was?" I panted suddenly breathless.

"Seventeen sixty-one," he repeated.

Seventeen sixty-one. December. Twenty-First. My legs grew weak and grey specks clouded my vision as I stared at him.

The same shirt, the same trousers.

The same.

Dear god. "You die today."

Chapter Twelve

Angus

Sobering was too kind a word for how my mind grew sharp at Nikki's words. I was nae sure when I started believing her, but I could always tell when someone was lying to me, and Nikki most certainly was nae lying. But how was any of it possible? Time travel? It was too fanciful to be believed. And yet, it was a magical time of year.

You ken you believe her, mo chridhe, Riona's voice said. *But about the Pride, perhaps you should go check on it.*

Riona was right as usual. I needed to go check on it. But could I? If Nikki was correct and I died that day would she be able to get back to her time? *How* would she be able to get back to her time?

"Well then," I began. "Perhaps we should get you home somehow."

"Angus, I can't leave you! Not today of all days!"

"You can and you will. I will not be responsible for your future changing. We need to figure out a way to get you home. In the future, did I have any ideas on that score?"

She shook her head. "None you shared with me."

I thought a moment. "You were found near the white heather," even though snow covered the ground I knew where my clan's flower was planted. I had surreptitiously planted some while Elizabeth was away in London six years ago. They bloomed every year. If I was to die that day, I would hope I would have some of those flowers on my grave and then I could sleep in peace under the Scottish symbol of my clan, my heart, my pride.

"The pump," she said.

I looked up at her. "The what, lass?"

"The pump it's where you were…"

"Where I was?" I questioned. She looked down. Ah, "Where I was buried?" She nodded. If I couldn't be with my family, then that was as good a place as any for my bones. "You say was, as in past tense."

She nodded. "When I found out where you were and was able to get you a pardon, um," she looked down as if worried she had said too much. "We were able to exhume you and bury you next to your father in the crypt."

"The crypt, it is safe?"

"Yes, the Scottish government granted me heir-rights and I was able to get everything protected."

"The Scottish government? So, Scotland is free in the future?" I asked, my heart light with the idea. But then her eyes clouded, and my stomach plummeted. "I see." I took a deep breath and let it out on a sigh. "Well, we need to find a way to get you home and if this... pump is the key then we will find a way."

"But it's not there," she said. "When I woke up this morning, I reached for it, and it wasn't there."

"What did it look like?"

"I only saw it once when it was new, it's fairly corroded and rusty in my time. But it has the MacPherson crest stamped on the pipe. And it was under the Ash tree near the white heather where I woke."

I had to chuckle. "I just received the order for a new kitchen pump yesterday. It is stamped with the MacPherson crest."

Nikki licked her lips, a tell she always did when something seemed too fantastic to be believed.

"Let me go up to my wife's room and get you something more appropriate to wear and then I will have Malcolm Brodie help me. I can trust him."

"Yes, you can," I smiled. "And Angus, he takes good care of Riona."

"Is she expecting?"

"She tells you today as you..."

"Lay dying?"

She nodded her head as tears gathered in her eyes. Suddenly, I felt a tightness in my own throat and a wetness around my lashes. I would never have another Christmas with my daughter. I would never hold my grandchild. *I die today.* Nikki closed her eyes and tears overflowed down her cheeks. I stood and unlocked the door to her prison. She launched herself at me and threw her arms around my neck as tears fell from her eyes.

"I don't want to go," she wept. "I can't leave you. Maybe you can live. Maybe you can write it all down and leave it for me to find. Maybe you don't have to die. We can figure it out."

"Lass," my voice thick around the knot in my throat. "My future is your past. It has already been written. I am grateful for these few moments with you. I am sorry for how I treated you when you first arrived."

"You didn't know. I didn't know. Nothing made sense. But I am so happy to be able to see you again. Hold you like this. I never thought I would again. It all works out in the end, Angus. You–"

I stopped her. "It is not for me to know, Lass. It is... Christmas magic. Cherish these few moments we have together. Not many people get this chance."

She rested her head on my chest and we stayed wrapped in each other's arms simply giving comfort for several minutes. She fit just like my late wife fit in my arms. Perfectly. This sweet, fiery, Scottish lass was my mark on the world. And I had a chance to meet her. I breathed in her soft rose scent and found my peace. I could go to my grave knowing I had this beautiful and strong young woman still fighting for me. With another deep breath, I let it out and with it all my fears and sadness.

"Stay here, lass," I whispered as I pulled away from her. "I will get you something to wear." She tugged me back for another embrace.

"Stay," she begged. "I haven't felt this safe in a bit."

That worried me. "But you said your fiancé..."

"Ross is wonderful," she said. "And I love him and feel safe with him. But we've been so busy, I fear we're drifting apart."

"Then you make time and fight for what you love. Donnae let life pass you by as you're watching from a safe distance. If you love this lad, you do everything you can to live. Life can change so quickly. You need to catch it and get ahead of it. Live like the sun may no' rise tomorrow because for some, it may no'."

She nodded into my chest.

"Now, let me go, lass," I said. "I will be right back." Again, she nodded and pulled away. Her tears had just barely dried. Leaving the door to the prison open, I hurried up the steps and came out in the corridor behind the walls. Weaving my way to the other side of the castle where our bedchambers were, I hoped Elizabeth would not be changing. I needed to find Nikki something to wear and get the pump installed.

Getting my mind distracted from my impending death helped but as I rounded the bend to the final stairs and passed the library, I heard voices coming through the wall. The old hidden Laird's Lug was fitted behind a bookshelf completely invisible unless you knew where to look. The voices were two I recognized immediately. My wife and her stepbrother. I inched forward and peered through the opening at eye level.

"He cannot find out, Crispin," Elizabeth said. "I have exactly what is needed. Tell the Cumberland I will have the Pride in a fortnight's time. The fool is transporting it but thinks I do not know."

So, it is true, I thought. *Elizabeth and Crispin are working together to steal the Pride.*

"Have you ever seen it?" Crispin asked.

"Not yet, but I know where it is," she answered.

"Just be careful," the man said. His voice had the same clipped English accent as Elizabeth. And it made me want to destroy everything he touched. Crispin reached forward and stroked her face. "I know we can never tell anyone, but you know how I feel," he went on. "Be careful."

My suspicions were confirmed. They were going behind my back and committing not only incest but adultery as well.

"Soon, my love," Elizabeth was saying. "Soon, all will be behind us. The legacy of the Stuarts will be crushed. They were far too weakened by Culloden, but Angus is too clever. He has kept the Pride safe and as soon as it is in the hands of the Hanover, we will be victorious, and we will be together."

"I love you, Elizabeth," Crispin said. "Just the thought of you giving yourself to that brute—"

Elizabeth silenced him with a kiss. My anger surged and I wanted nothing more than to break through the wall and kill them both. But I had no time. Elizabeth was right, I was transporting it. I wanted the Highland Pride safely in the Highlands. I had already spoken with The Sutherland and though the boy was only fifteen, he was as fierce as his father and grandfather.

The thought of Iain and Alastair Sutherland made me yearn for the way things used to be. My brother Niall, our friends, Scotland. Iain was like a second father to me, and Alastair was another brother. If Nikki's betrothed was anything like his forebears, he was a remarkable man indeed.

No time to further waste, I hurried to Elizabeth's room and discovered her maid had just left. That meant Elizabeth would soon be there to change for tea. Rushing to the wardrobe, I opened it and scanned through her clothing looking for something she did not wear often and therefore would not miss. Though, my hands paused on the red gown she wore for our portrait sitting that hung above her fireplace, if I did die that day, what difference would it make? And Nikki would look so beautiful in red.

Making my decision, I pulled the dress out of the wardrobe and was at the entrance to the secret passage before I heard the door open. No other decision, I tossed the dress into the secret passage and turned as Elizabeth entered.

"Oh there you are, Angus. I wanted to speak with you."

"Can it wait, Elizabeth? I am in the middle of something."

"No, it cannot wait," she answered.

Calming myself as I saw the defiance in her eyes, I nodded my head in acknowledgement for her to continue. She walked casually over to her seat by the window and picked up her embroidery.

"Crispin is here," she announced. "He arrived in time for tea."

"Aye," I growled. *I ken exactly what you and he were doing just a moment ago, too.* I thought it but no matter how much I wanted to say it, I could nae reveal Nikki's involvement nor the location of the Laird's Lug.

"He had news from Cumberland that his nephew, our King George, wants to expand his reach further north into the highlands. He has received word there is rich farmland up there and he needs someone to assist him."

"Expand his reach?" I questioned. "What does that mean?"

"It means, Angus," her tone and actions showed her thoughts of me. I was the lowliest of the low, a barbarian in her eyes and therefore could not understand. "That he wants you to help him establish a stronghold. He has his eye on Perth with further clearings. You have been chosen to assist the new king and I promised my brother that you would do whatever is necessary to bring honor to our house."

"More clearances?" I hated that word and began to pace.

"Of course," she answered. "The Scots needs to know and understand what happens when you have an uprising and lose."

I wanted to tell her exactly what would happen, but I refrained. My daughter's fate could rest on my silence.

"Very well," I stated. Apparently, I would not be alive to see it.

"Oh, and by the way, I have petitioned a meeting with his majesty."

"For what, if I may ask."

"For our marriage to be dissolved."

"Our... what?"

"It's not difficult to understand, Angus. We haven't been happy together in... well, have we ever? It's about time we both understand that fact, don't you think?"

"What are ye sayin', Elizabeth?" I demanded

"I'm saying I am leaving you, Angus," she replied slowly as if I was having a hard time understanding.

I stopped dead in my tracks and turned to stare at her.

"Why?" I breathed not contradicting her statement. She had never made me happy.

"I think I made myself perfectly clear," she answered. Her haughty tone and arrogance angered me even more.

"Hae I no' taken care of ye, lass?" I demanded. "Hae I no' given ye everythin' I hae?"

"You are a brute. I wish Father had never agreed to this marriage," Elizabeth answered.

"Ye were the one who wanted it!" I shouted. She seemed unfazed and kept embroidering. I was nae sure why I was arguing with her. "Ye'd shame me by leavin' my house?" I asked softer. "Ye've already shamed me by taking another to your bed."

"I have never loved you, Angus," she said. "This should come as no surprise to you."

Her words were like knives. When we were first married,

I was happy, happy to have a wife by my side and happy my daughter might have a mother but that changed on our wedding night. "Ye gut me, woman," I uttered. "Ye're my wife, before God and man. I'll no' be havin' ye leave my house."

"You knew I was no blushing bride when I married you, Angus," she replied. My eyes narrowed.

Aye, it was no secret I was nae her first but, "Ye were the one who seduced me!" I cried.

"Well, that should have told you right there I was no bonnie wee lassie," she mocked.

"Ye demanded yer father marry us!" I growled.

"Of course, you were but a pawn in my game," she grinned. If ever there was a witch... "It was so easy. You were pining for your dear dead wife. All I had to do was throw you a few little looks and get to your bedchamber. Tell me, did your wife take care of you like I did that night?"

Anger rose within me, rage like I had never felt. She dared speak of Riona. She dared speak of our love. As if my body had a story to tell without my permission, I stormed over to her and raised my hand to her. She put aside her needlepoint and stood up to face me defiantly.

"Go ahead, Angus," she taunted. "Do it. It will give me the proof I need of your brutality."

I froze, hand still raised, shaking with rage. After a moment, I calmed and lowered my hand.

"I have always tried to be a good husband to ye, Elizabeth," I finally whispered. "I hae ne'er hurt ye. I hae ne'er forced ye."

"I do not care what you call it," she said. "I only had you for my own pleasure. I am able to pick the men who have the potential to please me. You happened to be one of them. But now, you have failed. England will rule you and your precious Scotland for generations. You will never find the Highland Pride. I will make sure of it."

I took a foreboding step toward her. "Tha' is my family's property. Ye hae no right to it," I grasped her shoulders and shook.

"What are you going to do, Angus? Kill me for it?" she demanded.

"If I hae to," my voice was low as the temptation was nearly too much. Perhaps that was why I was buried under a pump and Nikki had to get me a pardon. Perhaps I killed her and therefore would not be buried in consecrated ground. "I hae ne'er raised hand nor whip to a woman apart from this day. I will nae abide an English spy in me midst. Nae me own wife," I spat. Her eyes widened only slightly, to anyone not trained in the art of the language your body gives it would have been imperceptible. "Och, aye, yer secret was nae well kept. I kenned when ye seduced me ye were working for Cumberland. Did ye think I was daft to no' ken what ye were doin'? Ye donnae become laird of yer clan by being taken in by a pretty face."

As realization dawned on her, she struggled to get free of me but my grip on her arms increased.

"Ye will nae shame me, lass. No English will e'er shame me. Ye ken the name I am kenned by. Take another to yer bed again and ye will both feel my wrath. I swear it, on me own grave, I will nae rest until I have had my revenge on ye. Ye stole something that belonged to me. I am a Highlander, lass, perhaps I should acquaint you with what that really means. As God is my witness, I will nae rest until the Pride is in my clan's hands once more."

"Let me go!" she screamed and pushed me away.

"You are free to go, madam, but remember my words." As I said the last, she raced out of the room.

I hurried to the secret passage, grabbing the red dress from the floor, and made my way back to Nikki.

When I offered the dress, Nikki stared at it for a long moment. "Something wrong?" I asked. Looking up at me, she shook her head, but I could tell something wasn't right. "Nikki?"

"It's just, that's the dress she wore in your portrait."

"Aye," I answered. "So you still have the painting?"

"No longer up, I refused to have that evil woman looking at me again."

"Again?" I questioned. She bit her lower lip as she clamped her mouth shut. "You should nae hae said tha', I assume?" She shook her head. If what Nikki let slip was true, Elizabeth would be joining me in the afterlife. I only prayed God was merciful and let me not be afflicted by her presence. "It's all right, lass. I will nae tell."

"We did have another portrait done," she said. "You were taken from the portrait with Elizabeth, but you were changed to wear your plaid and crest and I... I sat for Riona."

"Ah, lass that makes me verra happy. Now hurry, we must nae dawdle."

She nodded and I held up the dress as she slipped it on over her... workout clothes? Whatever that means. Helping with the ties, my clumsy fingers could barely tie them but somehow we got it to stay.

When she turned back to me, my breath caught. "Ye look beautiful, lass."

"Thank you," she said.

"Let's go."

"Angus," she stopped me once more. "I'm sorry."

"'Tis all right, lass," I said. "I know it seems two hundred and fifty years is a long time but knowing I have you to look forward to gives me some hope."

"I love you, Angus," she admitted.

"Ah, lass, then I can go to my death knowing that and it will give me comfort. But, I cannae leave you here if I am gone. Let's go now."

Taking her arm, I helped her up the steps and out to the back of the castle where she was found.

Chapter Thirteen

Nikki

The snow still covered the ground as we hurried. Angus helped me walk as the wind picked up again swirling snow in front of us. It was so hard to think of leaving, no matter how much I knew I had to and wanted to get back to my time but knowing when I left, Angus would be going to his death and everything that happened afterward, hurt my heart. There were no servants around as the shadows waned and darkness began to creep in. The setting sun glistened across the sky in red, orange, and pink colors. We reached the spot where Angus's pump stood in my time but still no pump.

"Malcolm has been called. He'll help me with the pump,"

Angus said. "We'll get you home, lass."

I looked over at him and took his hands. I didn't know how I knew but I had to walk through the trees on my own. It had nothing to do with the pump. I watched in fascination as the wolf appeared just at the tree line. He walked back and forth waiting for me.

"Angus," I began. "I know what I have to do. I feel it." I showed him the gooseflesh on my arms. He nodded. "I don't want to leave you, but I know it's what needs to happen."

"I will be fine, lass," he promised.

"You can't tell me any of this, okay?" I said. "If you say anything last year it won't happen how it's supposed to."

"I will nae," he swore. "Nikki, thank you for sharing my last day on this earth with me. Knowing I have you to look forward to, makes it so much easier."

Tears gathered in my eyes. "I was thinking of you just today and wishing I could see you again. This wasn't what I had in mind."

"Nay, I imagine no'," he smiled.

"But I am so grateful to be able to see you, hold you, talk to you again."

"I am glad for it too."

"Know this, your daughter is well taken care of, and you get to see her grow and see her children and grandchildren. Though they won't be able to see you, you will see them."

"That is a blessing."

"At home, we're getting ready for the Christmas holiday. Ross has the Yule Log ready to go and says we will be picking mistletoe today."

He smiled. "The old ways aren't lost, then. That's good." He looked around and smiled. "Look, lass." I followed his gaze. "Mistletoe." He squeezed my hand and walked over to it. Taking a knife from his trousers, he cut a piece off the tree and walked over to me. "Take it. Plant it so you have a part of me every year."

I took the plant, my eyes heavy with tears. "I don't want to leave you."

"I am sure Ross is worried sick about you, Nikki."

I looked up at him. "Do you think I can get through this?" Whatever *this* was, I wasn't certain, but I knew I needed to ask.

"You are a fighter, lass. You are a Scot. Always remember, yer a MacPherson and a Brodie and those two are a stubborn, tenacious but proud combination. Now go, lass."

I hugged him once more, taking a memory by breathing in his scent.

"Happy Christmas, Angus," I whispered.

"*Nollaig Chridheil*, lass," his softly rough voice caressed the Scots words, and his tone revealed the knot of emotion in his throat. Closing my eyes once more, I squeezed my arms around him and then let him go.

I looked up into his blue eyes, eyes I would never see again and let my tears fall.

"Goodbye, Nikki," he said.

"Goodbye, Angus. Thank you for always believing in me."

"Always, love."

With one final look at the man who appeared in my life and changed everything about it, I turned and began to walk, the wind picked up around me.

I glanced back to see him still standing there. He covered his chest with his open hand over where his heart beat, then pressed his fingers to his lips and blew me a kiss. I captured it with the one hand not holding my dress and kissed my fingers back to him.

I started to hear the wolf's panting as I neared the row of trees. The snow hung heavy on the branches as I crossed the hedgerow. The wolf walked over to me, and I stared down at him.

"Thank you, Angus," I said. "Get me home?"

The wolf nodded once and reared his head back, letting out a haunting howl. I closed my eyes as the darkness swirled and soon fell into nothingness.

Chapter Fourteen

Ross

"Where the hell is she?" I demanded. I was panicked now. It had been eight hours since I woke, and Nikki wasn't with me. The entire castle and village were out looking for her. "Please god, let her be all right." I just wanted her back. I wanted her in my arms. Safe.

We had walked the grounds six times and Travis; Nikki's father, had taken Mum and they drove around trying to see if anyone had seen her. The sun was setting, and I knew we wouldn't have enough light soon. But if they thought that would stop me, they had another thing coming. I would search for her forever if I had to.

I reached the row of trees for the seventh time, the castle before me. Letting out a roar, I fell to my knees and shouted to the heavens.

"Angus!" I bellowed. "If you can hear me, wherever you are, help me now! Please!"

Hanging my head, I tried to stop my thoughts. What if something bad had happened to her? What if someone took her? What if...

"Ross," I heard Angus' voice on the wind. "Look, lad."

Unsure how I heard his voice again, I obeyed and looked up. Angus's old pump stood to my left about ten yards away. But, I squinted. *What on earth? What is that?* The wind picked up suddenly swirling the snow around me making it difficult to see. Getting to my feet, I peered into the whiteout. There was something there. Either a very large something or two somethings. Either way, I shouted.

"Nikki!" My heart hammered in my chest as I trudged through the knee-deep snow, cursing my slowness. "Nikki," I shouted again.

One of the somethings moved. I was close enough to see two figures, one black and grey another in red. My heart stopped for a moment worried what sort of red it was. My stomach knotted at the thought I was too late.

"Frank! Chad!" I yelled for the two closest to me. At least I knew Frank was a doctor if Nikki was bleeding.

Finally close enough to see clearly, I froze when the massive head of a grey black wolf looked up at me. His crystal blue eyes watched me warily. I looked past it to the other figure. Nikki dressed in a blood red gown lying on her back in the snow. The wolf... next to her? Keeping her warm.

"Nikki?" I called again. She moaned, at least I think she did, the wind howled so loudly. The wolf looked at me and motioned his head. Then, it stood and walked two feet away. I raced as fast as I could to Nikki. She was pale but was moving. I crushed her to my chest. "Oh thank god! Nikki, Nikki can you hear me? Baby, can you open your eyes?"

"Ross!" I heard Chad shout.

"Over here!" Turning back to Nikki, I took in her body. She looked healthy, her tennis shoes poked out under the dress. "Nikki?"

"Ross?" I heard the sweetest sound. She moaned my name. "Ross?"

"I'm here, baby, I'm here."

"Angus," she breathed.

"Ang–" I looked over at the wolf still standing a couple feet away. "Angus?"

The wolf sat proudly and in the fading sunlight I saw a medallion around his neck. The MacPherson Crest. I gasped in disbelief.

"Angus, thank you for bringing her back to me," I said.

The wolf bowed his head and then, with a final look at Nikki who had sat up slowly in my arms and opened her eyes to watch, he turned and walked into the wind and snow disappearing from view. As soon as he vanished, the wind and snow stopped instantly. The eerie quiet set my teeth on edge but I held Nikki to me.

"Are you all right?" I questioned.

"Aye, I am, Ross," she smiled and licked her lips. "Angus says hello."

I let out a laugh and with it all the pent up fear. "I thought I lost you."

"Not with Angus around," she said. "You'll never lose me."

"Good," I leaned down and kissed her cold lips. My lips and face were practically numb, but it was the sweetest kiss I've ever had. "I love you."

"I love you too," she answered and wrapped her arms around my waist. Promptly shivering.

"Let's get you inside." Just as the words left my mouth, I heard Chad and Frank running as fast as they could toward me. Snow flying, their legs looking like they were hopscotching.

"Oh my god!" Chad shrieked falling to his knees next to me.

"Move Chadwick," Frank ordered and fell to my side as soon as Chad bounded out of the way. "Nikki, can you hear us?" She nodded. "Tell me, is there anywhere you don't have feeling?" She shook her head. "We need to get you inside and warmed. Ross," he stated as if asking if I would carry her. At my agreement, Frank helped Chad up from a snow drift he landed in when he hurried to move. "Run on ahead and make sure there's a roaring fire lit in the library bar. Bring down towels, lots of towels and a complete change of clothes for her. Sweats preferably. Also put on some hot tea." Chad nodded and took off running, or hopscotching, through the foot and a half of snow. Frank stayed with me and helped me carry Nikki.

"Really, I'm okay, just a little cold," Nikki said.

"It's been hours, Nikki. I'm going to check and make sure you don't have hypothermia or at best frostbite," Frank stated.

"Someone needs to call the others," I reminded him.

"You or Chad can do that as soon as you set her down. I'll look after her. I'll need to check her as she changes anyway."

I agreed and hurried into the house, carrying the love of my life in my arms. Heading straight for the library bar to see Chad had stoked the fire and added some more logs as well as set out blankets. I didn't see him and assumed he was doing the rest of what Frank asked him to do. I set Nikki on the sofa just as she started shivering.

"Good, that's a good sign," Frank said kneeling before her as he started pulling at the ties of the gown. "How long have you had this on?"

"I... I don't know," she answered. She looked up at me, but I couldn't interpret her expression.

Frank pulled off her shoes and socks and then helped her with the dress just as Chad raced in, arms laden with towels and clothes.

"I just grabbed whatever I could find. I think the sweats might be yours, Ross," he said.

"It's fine," I replied. As much as I wanted to take Nikki into my arms, I stayed back to let Frank work. Sending a text to the group search party to let them know Nikki was found and safe, I hurried to help Frank. Nikki's color was returning and as soon as she was changed into clean dry clothes, I sat beside her and took her into my arms.

"Body heat is the best thing," Frank said. "But you seem to be doing fairly well."

"Thanks, Frank," she replied.

"What the hell happened?" Chad demanded. Now she was out of danger, I could see he was scared.

"I don't honestly know," she answered.

Just as she said that everyone poured into the room. Her dad raced to her side as our friends gathered around to see for themselves that she was all right. The clatter was loud for her, I could tell by the way she winced as everyone talked over everyone else. Chad handed her a cup of tea and Frank ordered her to sip it.

"Hey, everyone," I called. "Let's take it down a notch. Nikki will tell us what happened in her own time. Let's give her some room."

"So glad you're okay, sweetie," Jess said as she squeezed her hand and then walked over to Graeme. Jenn and James offered their support and happiness that she was all right, then moved to one side too. Of course, Travis wasn't going anywhere, and I wouldn't ask him too. He sat on Nikki's other side and wrapped his arm around her.

"Thank god, babe, hypothermia is no joke," Brit stated, then shyly glanced at Gerard who locked eyes with her and subtly reached his hand out to her. She walked over to him and took it.

Once everyone had said their piece, I turned to Nikki. "Can you tell us what happened, baby?"

Nikki nodded. "I'm not sure I believe it myself, but it is the truth."

She launched into the story and honestly I was drawn in. When she revealed that the dress was in fact the one in Elizabeth's portrait, it all made sense.

"Wow, so is he like, back?" Jess asked.

"No," Nikki answered. "No, he's gone, but it was my Christmas wish to see him again. I just didn't expect it to be like that."

"And he was going to his death?" Marilyn asked.

Nikki's face screwed up as tears threatened. "And I couldn't do anything."

"Hey, you did. You did more than you think. You gave him something to look forward to. Just think, he was waiting for you, Nikki. He knew. He knew it all before you even arrived," I tried to offer her some peace. "You gave him hope."

"You did, honey," Chad said. "And just to know there's something beyond? That's hope for anyone about to die." He looked up at his husband who placed a comforting hand on his shoulder. "It was a Christmas miracle, revel in that."

"You're right," she replied. "I knew I wouldn't be able to change anything, but it was so good to see him again. He really helped me through some difficult decisions, and I'll always be grateful for that."

"What difficult decisions?" I asked.

She looked up at me and smiled. "Marry me."

I looked at her surprised. "Ehm, we already are planning it, baby."

"No, I mean marry me. Today. Right now. I don't want to wait. We have everyone here that we love, and I don't want to let life pass me by. I want to get ahead of it and catch it. You are my future, Ross Sutherland. I don't want to wait. Will you marry me? Today? Right now?"

I breathed a laugh but had no other answer than, "yes, love, in a heartbeat but don't you want your big wedding? Church, reception, honeymoon?"

"Oh, I expect a honeymoon, Sutherland," she teased. "And maybe we can have the reception as a celebration, but I don't want to wait another minute to call you husband."

"Then absolutely, Nikki," I answered. Looking around the room, I asked. "Anyone here ordained?"

"I got ordained online last year for a friend's wedding," James offered. "I'd be happy to officiate."

I grinned then turned to my soon-to-be wife. "Then Nicole Thompson, on this Silent night, let's get married." Nikki grinned and lunged forward kissing me.

"We haven't gotten to that part yet," James teased.

"You know I'm doing this for you, honey," Chad said. "I had

an outfit all picked out and you're forcing me to wear something I brought?"

"We could always make it an ugly Christmas sweater theme..." She said.

"No, that's not happening," I winked. "If you don't mind a kilt, Chad, I have several from which to choose."

"I have the legs for that," Chad grinned. "Deal."

After changing into something a bit more appropriate, Nikki and I met our friends and family in the library bar where it all began over a year ago. I had my two best friends with me, my fiancée had her two best friends with her. Her father walked her down the aisle. She had a sprig of fresh mistletoe in her bouquet of roses and pinecones. She wore the red dress Angus had given her with my green, blue, red and white striped tartan sash over her shoulder and my mother's old broach holding it in place. Something old, something new, something borrowed, something blue.

My mother, Marilyn, Chad, Frank, and Jenn all looked on with happy smiles glowing in the twinkle lights of the Christmas tree.

As I made my vows to the woman I loved, and heard her vows to me in return, I knew nothing would ever compare to how I felt at that moment. When James pronounced us husband and wife, I kissed the woman I was lucky enough to be spending the rest of my life with and thanked a certain Scottish Ghost who haunted my castle looking for the Highland Pride, for bringing us together.

The End

Acknowledgements

Thank you! Thank you! I want to thank all of you who helped make the first book, *Silent Whispers* a success! I hope you enjoyed *Silent Night* as much as I did writing it. It is always fun to revisit characters from previous books especially at the most wonderful time of the year and Ross, Nikki, and Angus hold a special place in my heart!

I want to thank my beta readers and editor for another amazing job! I couldn't have done it without you.

I look forward to 2022 and the next books to be released! Be sure to follow me on social media under the handle M. Katherine Clark Author for the latest information on my next books. I have a lot of fun ideas coming soon! If you enjoyed this book, please consider writing a review on your favorite book website!

I hope you all have a wonderful Christmas and holiday season! If you enjoyed the paranormal wolf side of this book, please read on for a look at my paranormal suspense series; *The Wolf's Bane Saga!* The complete series is now available on eBook and paperback, audio coming soon.

Thanks for revisiting MacCulloch Castle with me and *Nollaig Chridheil - Merry Christmas!*

The Wolf's Bane Saga

Book One

Wolf's Bane

M. KATHERINE CLARK

Legend has it, that before the Romans invaded Britannia in 55 B.C. the people of that land roamed wild and free. Once the Roman legionnaires pushed back the wild and untamed Celts, they built a wall; Antonine's Wall. It was once magnificent, once imposing... trust me, I was there, I saw it.

But was it the humans they feared... or us?

There are so few of us left. But under the Hunter's Moon, we lived, and we died, and this is the story of both.

Chapter One

Aberlyall north of Aberdeen, Scotland – 650 A.D.

Alexina's trained ears heard it before the rest of her family. Piercing the silence of the wintery night, was a long, low wolf howl in the woods behind their house.

"The wolves are coming closer," her father said gruffly, stoking the fire and touching the long knife tied to his leg.

"Afton was saying that the Hunter's Moon is supposed to shine within the week. He said the wolves come down to the village and kill *everyone* that night. Is it true they can rip your heart out with one strike?" Alexina's ten-year-old brother, Niels asked.

"Och nay," their twelve-year-old brother, Harailt, said. "They are much stronger than that. They can take your *head* off in a single blow."

Niels leaned over and clutched their mother's leg, frightened.

"Harailt, donnae scare your brother like that," their mother said as she sat knitting beside her husband.

"We have nothing to worry about," their father said. "This town is well protected by the wolf's bane that grows in every garden," he indicated the purple flower that hung above the door like a garland. "Never leave the house without it," he tapped near to where a flower was pinned to his tunic. "And *never* go into the woods," their father warned just as another howl rippled from the wolf outside.

"What about real wolves?" Niels whispered almost afraid the wolf would hear him. "Afton's father says 'tis easy to tell them apart."

"According to legend," their father began, "you can tell those born naturally from the yellowed-eyed demons due to their size. If you see a smaller wolf, you should never engage with it, but you are safer than you would be if you met one of *them*. But, the wolf-men have killed practically all of them anyway. They are nothing but animals," he spat.

Alexina looked down and breathed deeply. Normally their times before the fire were filled with tales and legends but with the Hunter's Moon approaching, the only things she heard in the village were the tales of the yellow-eyed demons and their perverse ways. Even her much younger siblings had heard of them. Nearing her eighteenth year, Alexina had heard all of the stories and half of them were too fanciful to be believed.

"You are rather quiet, Alexi," her mother said eyeing her over her knitting. Alexina looked up sharply afraid her secret was known. "Are you all right?"

"Actually, mama, my head aches. May I go to my room?" Alexina asked.

"Of course, dear," she replied as her daughter stood from the floor. "I have feverfew if you require it."

"Och nay," Alexina said rubbing her temples. Her light brown hair was pulled away from her face in a braid around her head. "Thank you, 'tis nothing a rest will nae cure. Goodnight," she called.

She walked slowly to her room and closed the door. The second the door was closed, she hurried to her bed and placed the pillows under the furs to show her outline. Then she rushed to her chest and took out her brown cape. Pulling it on, she raced to the window and threw open the shutters. She eased out of the house and pulled her hood over her head. Running toward the edge of the woods, the sound of the dead leaves that had fallen earlier that month, crunched beneath her soft leather clad feet. Every step and sound made her flinch, thinking it would give her away to her family.

The snow blanketed the ground and made the Highlands glow white under the moon. She hardly felt the chill as she walked. Reaching the edge of the woods, Alexina looked back to the cottage. The smoke from the peat fire still billowed out of the chimney. There was no movement inside, her family did not know she had left.

She ducked into the forest just as another wolf howl ripped through the silence of the night.

Weylyn's yellow wolf eyes flew open when he heard the door to his hut creak and close softly. He stayed exactly how he was, resting on his side, his back to the door. Sniffing the room, the familiar scent of his pupil filled his nostrils.

"Where have you been?" Weylyn asked softly, not moving.

"Gods above, Weylyn, you startled me," Tristan breathed. "I thought you were asleep."

Turning over, Weylyn sat up and looked at him, his eyes back to the brown color of his human form.

"I ask you again, where have you been?" Weylyn asked.

"Out in the forest," Tristan answered simply, not meeting his mentor's eyes.

"You were with that human lass again," Weylyn said standing.

"Nay, I was no'," he replied shuffling towards his own bed.

Weylyn took a deep breath, smelling the scents that surrounded his student.

"Donnae lie to me, Tristan," he replied gently.

"So what if I was," Tristan turned to his cot and pulled off his cloak.

"She is nae of our kind. She will nae understand," Weylyn said.

"She does. She does understand," Tristan replied finally looking up at him.

"A relationship with a human is nae a good idea, trust me," Weylyn stressed. "When your father finds out—"

"You are nae going to tell him!" Tristan stepped towards him, panicked.

"Nay," Weylyn replied calming him. "No' as long as I have your promise that you will never see her again."

Tristan stared at him for a long moment, searching his face for something. Finally, he lowered his head and nodded once.

"I promise," he swore.

"You are lying," Weylyn replied simply.

Tristan locked eyes with his mentor. "I love her," he breathed.

Weylyn closed his eyes for a moment, an unpleasant memory coming back to him. When he opened his eyes, he looked at his young student. Tristan, his dark blonde hair was not quite long enough to be tied back, his deep brown eyes were pleading with him. The male looked twenty-five but was actually seventy years old in wolf years and was still a boy in so many ways. In human years, he would have only been nineteen.

Weylyn breathed deeply. *Dear gods, is this what my father felt?* He wondered. Hating that he had to advise Tristan away from a love Weylyn knew first hand was stronger than any other bond; he could not let Tristan go through the pain that he had felt all those years ago... Weylyn shook his head clearing it. *Donnae think on it,* he thought to himself. *It is in the past... there is nothing you can do but save him from the absolute heart wrenching ache that you felt.*

"Does she ken what you are?" Weylyn asked treading lightly.

"Aye and she does nae care," he answered.

"Have you mated with her?" Weylyn asked.

Tristan looked at him, sharply.

"Nay," he breathed truthfully. "We have no'."

Weylyn breathed a sigh of relief.

"All is no' lost then," he whispered.

"But we plan on getting married," Tristan replied. "Human married, no' wolf, with her family's blessing and with witnesses. She thinks she can convince her parents to meet me and rid their cottage of wolf's bane."

"If you do this, you will be cast out of the pack, or killed. You ken what that means?" Weylyn asked. "Is she really worth it?"

"You tell me," Tristan replied heatedly. "I ken you loved a human once. Was she worth it? You left her!"

"You donnae ken of what you speak," Weylyn said feeling an old wound reopening in his chest.

"Do I no'?" Tristan asked harshly. "I am no' a child, Weylyn! I ken what I want, and I am more of a male than you are! I will nae let anything stand in the way of my love! You left yours out in the cold and she died carrying another male's child. Can you honestly tell me that your course is better than mine? Alexina and I will be married. We will mate. And we will live together forever! She will be mine! She is mine! And I love her, which is more than you can say!"

Weylyn's hand swiped across Tristan's face in a hard slap. Tristan turned back to his mentor; his eyes yellowed, his hair falling in his face, his teeth barred, his body growing taller and his muscles tightening ready to pounce in a half-phase. Tristan's upper lip was pulled back as he growled and snapped at him.

"Calm down," Weylyn ordered still in his full human form.

Tristan's lip lifted on one side as he snarled.

"You cannae stop me," he said his voice rough, the sound vibrating in his chest in a half-phased growl. "Face me."

"I will nae," Weylyn replied calmly.

"Coward," Tristan roared and pounced on him.

Even though Weylyn had not phased, he was still able to throw Tristan off him. Tristan attacked in anger and even though Weylyn's heart was breaking again after so many years, he still was able to remain calm.

The boy stood back up from the corner where Weylyn had thrown him and Weylyn's body convulsed into a half-phase. The wolf men faced each other, their teeth barred and their eyes staring into each other's. Their chests heaved as they panted. Their bodies ached anticipating a fight.

Finally, almost as if Tristan realized what he was doing, he backed down and phased to his full human form. Weylyn did the same.

"I am sorry," Tristan said. "I did nae mean to fight you." Weylyn nodded once, accepting his apology.

"I am sorry for striking you," Weylyn replied.

"I deserved it," Tristan answered. "I did nae mean to hurt you with my words. You are right. I donnae ken anything about what happened between you and your mate, I only ken what you told me. And I am truly sorry for it. But I love Alexina."

"I understand that," Weylyn started gently. "And I am glad you were able to experience that sort of love, but for your own sake, you must think of your father and your position. You are to be Alpha. You must understand the ramifications of what you are doing. Trust me; I ken how strong the pull is. But you have to understand that even if you do marry this human girl, you ken your father," he stressed, stepping towards him and placing his hands on Tristan's shoulders. "Marrock will hunt you both down and the gods only ken what he will do to you, no' to mention her family, when he finds you. If you love her, the best thing for her would be for you to let her go."

They were both quiet for a long time, Tristan staring at his mentor hearing the truth and the weight of his words. Eventually, Tristan nodded.

"You are right," he said. "I cannae do that to her. I will tell her in the morning."

Weylyn saw something flash in his pupil's eyes, but decided to ignore it, hoping Tristan's history with his father would prove incentive enough.

"Get some sleep, everything will be all right in the morning," Weylyn finally said.

"You are right," Tristan mumbled turning to his cot. "Things will be different in the morning."

Weylyn awoke to an annoying bird chirping right outside the window that was just above his bed. He growled and it flew off. Stretching, he breathed in the early morning air and smelled the threatening snow. It had been a harsh winter for the villages near them and Weylyn knew they could not handle another snowstorm. If the repairs he had helped with were any indication, Weylyn was certain another large snow fall would be detrimental.

Pulling his tunic over his head, he tightened the strings of the *leine* just at his neck. Slowly he stood and stretched again. Looking over at Tristan's cot, he saw the outline of his student still there under the blankets. Not wishing to disturb him after the emotional encounter late last night, Weylyn took a deep breath.

Tristan's scent was faint. Concerned, Weylyn went over to his cot.

"Tristan?" He called softly. There was no movement. Weylyn touched the place where his student's shoulder should have been. Confused, he pulled down the blanket slowly. He yanked it back when he saw what was beneath. Several pillows were placed strategically to show the outline of a body, but Tristan was not there.

Weylyn convulsed into a half-phase and sniffed the air. Tristan's scent was very faint. He had been gone a few hours. Weylyn growled.

How could I have been so blind? He thought, angry with himself. He knew Tristan was going to leave and he did nothing to stop him. *Where is he?* Weylyn saw a folded note resting on the pillow. His name was scripted across it in Tristan's hand. He phased back into his human form and picked it up.

Weylyn,

I am sorry. I love her too much to live without her. Please understand. I would rather spend what little time I have with her than a hundred years alone. Please wait to tell my father until the sun is at its peak; it will give us enough time to get away. I ken I have nae right to ask this, but I have always felt, you loved me as a son. Please, I beg of you, donnae raise the alarm. We are going far enough away, somewhere he will no' find us.

Forgive me, my dear friend, but I have seen what it has done to you no' being with your mate and I cannae let that happen to me. I was wrong last night; I am no' more of a male than you. I realize that now. You have had to live without her for over forty years. You have survived. Whereas I am very selfish, I refuse to live without her at all. Forgive what I said last night, it was from anger, and I did nae understand. I pray you donnae suffer for my selfishness and I hope we will meet again. This is no' on you. This is my choice.

Goodbye, my friend. You have been more of a father to me than my own blood. Thank you and be at peace.

Tristan

"Fool," Weylyn breathed rubbing his eyes with his fingers and pinching the bridge of his nose.

There was a sharp knock at his door and Weylyn looked up suddenly. He folded the note and threw it into the fire before him. Turning back to Tristan's cot, he removed the pillows. Straightening it as best he could to look like Tristan had awakened earlier and made his bed, Weylyn glanced back into the fire and saw that the note was completely charred then went to answer the door.

"My king," he bowed low when he saw Marrock, his Alpha and Tristan's father, standing in front of him. "Please come in. Forgive me for keeping you waiting. I slept poorly last night and was still recovering."

"Weylyn," Marrock nodded, lowering his head as he stepped through the low threshold. "Leave us," he said to his guards. They bowed and walked away. The small hut was dwarfed by Marrock's mighty frame. He was the biggest of them all. Marrock's black hair was longer than Weylyn's and unbound. His light eyes scanned the room and landed on his son's empty cot.

"To what do I owe this great honor, Sire?" Weylyn asked after shutting the door behind his Alpha.

"I wanted to see how things were progressing," Marrock said. "I wanted to come and speak with you without my son here. I suppose he has gone out early?" Weylyn nodded not knowing what to say. Remembering that Marrock hardly visited his son after the death of his first wife and Tristan's mother, Weylyn knew Marrock wished to speak with him alone. "Good, now tell me, have you been able to get these ridiculous notions out of my son's head?"

"The notion that all men are created equal, sire?" Weylyn clarified holding back his scorn for his Alpha's request. Weylyn believed in that *ridiculous notion* as well. "Unfortunately, your son still holds to his convictions on that."

"What about his inane notion we should live at peace with the humans?" Marrock asked chuckling as he spoke.

"That one, sire, I *have* been able to discuss with him," Weylyn replied but, knowing where Tristan was at that moment, it seemed like a fruitless discussion.

"Good," Marrock replied. "I was nae too sure if you were the correct choice to instruct my son regarding that considering your history with the human race. But I kenned you could nae refuse me."

"Nay, sire," he answered lowering his eyes. "I believe I have made that perfectly clear in the past."

"Aye" he replied smirking. "Good..." he turned to the empty cot. "Well, where is he?"

"Tristan?" He said.

"I was nae asking after the servants," Marrock replied smoothly.

"He... um... went out early," Weylyn said.

"Tell me the truth," Marrock's alpha order made Weylyn quake. He could not prevent his answer; he could however give him only part of the truth.

"He left early, sire," he said. "He woke and went for a walk."

"A walk?" Marrock asked enjoying seeing Weylyn quake at his command. "Where?"

"I donnae ken, sire," he said. "Tristan likes to be alone with his thoughts."

"Hmm," Marrock answered walking around and smelling for his scent. "He has been gone for a while now."

"I donnae ken, sire, as I said I had a difficult night and was no' awake when he left," Weylyn explained.

"I see," Marrock went on. "Well, when he returns tell him I want to see him."

"Uh – of – of course," he replied bowing. Marrock never asked to see his son. Nodding once, Marrock left without another word. Weylyn waited until he saw Marrock outside through the window near his bed. He was walking back towards the keep with his guards. "Oh, Tristan, you fool." Weylyn sighed softly looking back at the cot and closing his eyes for a moment.